Five yards, Alex. Maggie's as desperate as you are. Her stroke has disintegrated a bit. Her mother is frozen, still as a stone, white-faced. She thinks it's all over.

My stroke went out the window ages ago. I feel like some sort of crazy windmill.

Looks good to me. I've always loved watching you swim, Alex, the sheer power of you. I get the same feeling watching dolphins in the sea out from the beach.

I was thinking of dolphins earlier.

Wait till afterwards, concentrate on what you're doing. Three yards, Alex, she thinks she's got you . . .

Andy, help me, please . . . I want, so badly . . . to win.

Other Bantam Starfire books you will enjoy

In Lane Three, Alex Archer

Tessa Duder

BANTAM BOOKS
NEW YORK • TORONTO • LONDON • SYDNEY • AUCKLAND

The assistance of the
Children's Publication Fund
is gratefully acknowledged.

RL 6, age 12 and up

*This edition contains the complete text
of the original hardcover edition.*
NOT ONE WORD HAS BEEN OMITTED.

IN LANE THREE, ALEX ARCHER

*A Bantam Book / published by arrangement with
Houghton Mifflin Company*

PRINTING HISTORY
*Houghton Mifflin edition published 1989
Bantam edition / June 1991*

*The Starfire logo is a registered trademark of Bantam Books,
a division of Bantam Doubleday Dell Publishing Group, Inc.
Registered in U.S. Patent and Trademark Office and elsewhere.*

*Bantam Books are published by Bantam Books, a division of
Bantam Doubleday Dell Publishing Group, Inc. Its trademark,
consisting of the words "Bantam Books" and the portrayal of a
rooster, is Registered in U.S. Patent and Trademark Office and in
other countries. Marca Registrada. Bantam Books, 666 Fifth Avenue,
New York, New York 10103.*

PRINTED IN THE UNITED STATES OF AMERICA

OPM   0   9   8   7   6   5   4   3

Contents

Author's Note

Anyone familiar with the fine sport of swimming in New Zealand during the period described will detect some historical liberties. For dramatic reasons, the locations of championship meetings during the period have been slightly changed, and for reasons of simplicity race distances have been given in imperial measurements.

New Zealand school students sat School Certificate around age fifteen, at the end of the Fifth Form, and the following year were either accredited or required to sit the Sixth Form examination of University Entrance.

Passing reference is made to some of the outstanding champions of the time—the Australian freestyle swimmers Dawn Fraser, Lorraine Crapp, Jon and Ilse Konrads, the English backstrokers Judy Grinham and Margaret Edwards. Apart from these, all characters are entirely fictitious.

Prologue

I have always known that in another life I was—or
will be—a dolphin. I'm silver and grey, the sleekest
thing on fins, with a permanent smile on my face. I
leap over and through the waves. I choose a passing
yacht to dive under and hear the shouts of the children as I emerge triumphant close to the boat.

Right at this moment, I'd give anything for that
freedom. I am a pink human, caught in a net of
ambition and years of hard work. In a few minutes I
will dive into that artificially turquoise water waiting
at my feet. A minute later I'll be either ecstatic or a
failure.

I stare at my toes, which are white with fright.
How will I ever get my legs going with feet of mar-
ble? I step from one foot to the other. My arms
describe drunken windmills. I'll need all the oxygen I
can get: I breathe in long slow lungfuls. My heart is
already pumping away as if it has gone berserk.

I hear 'In Lane three, Alexandra Archer' and something else, which is lost in cheers. Automatically I
step on to the starting-block. 'In Lane four, Maggie
Benton,' in the lane I wanted to be in, should have
been in. Cheers and shouts for her, too. More than
for me, or less? I have never been able to tell. What
does it matter, anyway? I stand head down. Nothing

will make me look at her. Since we hugged goodbye this morning we have avoided each other, carefully not being in the dressing-room at the same time, not meeting in doorways, sitting well apart in the competitors' enclosure. I hope she is feeling as ghastly as me.

We all step down. I walk back to the chair where a woman in a blazer waits to take my track suit. My hands are shaking so much that I can't get my fingers latched on to the tab of the zip. She helps me. Yes, I did put my swimsuit on under all this, my most special pair. People haven't, in the past, from nerves.

Then comes the gold chain, bearing my most precious possession in all the world, Andy's pearl, his tear. It goes deep into my track suit pocket, along with his parents' telegram.

I'm cold, so cold . . . appalled at what I have to do. I stand tall, centre stage, on the first rung of the starting-block. Under the night sky, I feel almost naked. Just me, the body Alex, fit, ready, dangerous.

A whistle blows somewhere. I climb up to the block, as to a guillotine. Shouts and cheers echo around the packed stands. 'Maggie', 'Alex', 'Come on, Maggie', 'Go Alex'. Then, silence falls like a curtain.

I make a last adjustment to the cap clinging to my ears, a last swing of the arms, shake of the feet, shrug of the shoulders. I hear the breakers of my nightmares crash on the nearby beach. I need a pee.

'Take your marks.'

I curl my toes carefully around the edge of the block. It's a relief to bend my knees. I crouch down, *hearing the wrench of cartilage in knee joints, and look along the fifty-five yards of smooth blue water in front of me. Up and back we'll go, flat out. I feel tired already.*

Heads or tails? This throw is for you, Andy.

Beside me someone starts to move.

Bang!

Alex, you're dead.

Maggie's got a flyer on you. A glorious flyer. You're beaten before you even start.

1

It all began years ago. I'm a veteran at fifteen years and two and a half months, a seasoned campaigner with countless races under my belt, and the subject of much journalistic purple prose, which charts my ups and downs. This last year, it was mostly downs. Those reporters have had a field day with Maggie and me! And how I get it in the neck at school when they write something!

Monday last week was bad, the worst yet. Start of a new term, a new year, everyone at school, frisky with holiday gossip and sizing up the new teachers. A long piece on Maggie and me appeared in the morning paper. I'd biked along to the pool, done my usual training, and come home sodden with pool water, eyes a delicate shade of pink, to peaches and cereal, steaming bacon and eggs with fried potato, four slices of toast, and hot chocolate to drink. Try doing two and a half miles' hard swimming before breakfast and you'd need more than a cup of coffee, too.

Dad waited until I'd finished my last bit of toast, and the others had all been shooed off to get ready for school. 'You'd better have a look at this.'

'Look at what?'

'Remember that reporter from the women's page? Came to see you last week.'

'The orange sack dress, and very high stilettoes?'

'That's her. Here's the result.' He handed me the paper. I didn't like the expression in his eyes. 'Did she tell you she was going to see Maggie as well?'

'No, she did not.'

My eyes were still blurred with chlorine. Through the haze I recognized a ghastly photo of myself taken by the photographer who'd sat in the armchair picking his teeth and reading a book, while his wig-wearing mate had asked her silly questions. Then he asked me to sit on the verandah with the family dog in a stupid Hollywood starlet pose, and when I refused, he got all surly and grumpily fired a few flashbulbs. It wasn't a bad picture of the dog, or of the verandah.

Silly questions get silly answers. What had possessed me to answer them? Or had I, indeed? The reporter hadn't been taking shorthand, I'd noticed that much.

'SWIMMERS HAVE FEMININE INTERESTS TOO!' the headline proclaimed. I looked up at Dad. He was studiously marmalading his toast. Over at the bench, both Gran washing dishes and Mum cutting lunches had their backs turned, but I knew they were listening and waiting.

'Life is not all stop-watches for Auckland's two brilliant girl swimmers who meet at the national championships in Napier next week to settle which of them goes to the Rome Olympic Games in August.

'Despite their gruelling training programmes, which

5

mean four hours a day in the pool, fifteen-year-old Maggie Benton and her great rival of many years, Alexandra Archer, retain their interest in more traditional feminine matters.'

(Maggie first, again. Well, that's fair enough. Maggie's the famous one, I'm more what you'd call notorious. Nevertheless . . .)

A spiel about the pretty, slim Maggie followed, about her dark gamin hairstyle, which suits a swimmer's life as well as being very stylish, her love of nice clothes, her devoted mother and immaculate house full of interesting Eastern curios, her cute younger sister and her father an importer. 'Maggie wishes she had more time for boyfriends and parties, but enjoys going to the movies, reading, sewing her own dresses, listening to Elvis and Pat Boone records, and reading *Seventeen* magazines.' Her photo showed her doing just that, with devoted mother (fresh from the hairdresser) peering proudly down from behind. 'Eventually she wants to do a secretarial course, maybe some modelling, and travel. Maybe she will do something connected with the tourist industry, since she was brought up in Singapore and has travelled with her parents around Asia and Australia.'

Of course, we all want to travel. Now Maggie may be the person I most want to beat in this entire world (perhaps for the equal pleasure of beating her mother), but I actually like her. She's shy rather than stand-offish, quite funny when she gets going, and certainly not the 'yes-Mother-no-Mother' little drip I once thought. And she's always been generous on those occasions when I have beaten her, and she's not nearly *that* gormless.

'And what about her arch-rival, Alex Archer, who is also vying for the Olympic nomination? "Alex and I get on quite well out of the water," says Miss Benton. "But I suppose I must have a killer instinct that comes to the fore when we line up for an important race." (What a load of rubbish. Maggie just swims, she always has. She is more interested in times than beating people. And no one our age talks like that.) Mrs Harold Benton, her attractive youthful mother, listening proudly to her acclaimed daughter, adds, "Maggie has a wonderful race temperament. She is very calm and determined. We are feeling very confident about the championships next week and the Olympic nomination that will follow." '

The hell it will. With dread, I came to my part. According to the reporter, I live in a comfortable old house where I am the eldest of four children. My mother, Mrs James Archer, a devoted 'home-maker', works hard to provide the extra big meals that I need, lots of steak and vitamin C. (Translation: big girls need feeding up.) My grandmother, Mrs Albert Young, lives in a bed-sitting-room especially built on for her. She tends the large vegetable garden and chicken-run out the back, and sews our clothes. Father works in the Post Office. He was a fine swimmer and tennis player in his day, a backstroke champion. The younger children (James 12, Debbie 9 and Robert 4) are all proud of their famous big sister. My parents are pleased with my achievements, but try to encourage the other children as well, and my activities do not run the entire household. (I'll say!)

The next bit made me choke. 'Besides her swimming prowess, Alex is an outstanding senior student and a prefect at her school. This year she hopes to qualify for university entrance. She represents the school in hockey, and takes a leading role in school theatrical productions as a talented musician and dancer, having passed advanced examinations in piano and ballet. She has temporarily suspended most of her other activities outside school hours to concentrate on her bid for Olympic nomination. Her training regimen includes calisthenics and weights, which she greatly enjoys. She says she has not yet decided on her future, but one possibility is the study of law. Or perhaps she'll "just get married and have lots of children."'

I looked up into Dad's eyes. He'd been waiting for me to get to that bit.

'Just get married! Just get . . . what! I never said anything of the sort.'

'You didn't?'

'I most certainly did not.' I tried to remember what I had said. '*She* asked me if I might get married and have children and was I worried about having big shoulders and difficult childbirth after having done so much sport. I said of course not, I'm a fit healthy female, what more did doctors want? And one day I might get married and I might have kids *if* I felt like it. Then I said it was a myth that girl swimmers got big shoulders. They were swimmers because they had strong shoulders in the first place,

8

although not all, you only have to look at Maggie. She's only five foot five, even if she has got hands like paddles and takes two sizes bigger than me in shoes. And both my parents were tall so it was hardly surprising that I was five foot ten and one-quarter and you're quite tall yourself and do people ask you about difficult childbirth all the time. She looked a bit po-faced at that.'

Over at the sink, Gran was chuckling away. 'No wonder she's giving you a hard time,' she said.

But Dad wasn't smiling. 'Alex, I thought you'd have learned by now. The less you say to reporters the better.'

This time I didn't merely choke. I stood up, knocking over the chair, waving the paper with rage. 'Listen to this. "Miss Archer, who is five foot ten and of Junoesque proportions, says she misses the parties and dances and movie-going that her school contemporaries enjoy. 'Most of the boys I meet,' she says, 'seem rather scared of me.' " '

'You said *that?*' asked Mum, wiping down the table.

'It wasn't. I didn't. Gran, stop laughing, please. She . . . she asked me all those stupid questions and I said yes and no and I suppose so and maybe sometimes. I did not *say* them. Well, I wasn't going to tell her about Andy, was I, or those other things? Once upon a time, there was a very tall princess who had a very tall boyfriend called Andy . . . Heck, Dad, she did all the talking, then she turned it all around. I don't even know what Junoesque means. I bet it's something rude.'

'Junoesque? Tall, stately. Juno was . . . who was Juno, Helena?'

'Roman goddess, consort of Jupiter, the Roman god of victory.' My mother is a lady of few words, but she knows a lot. It's all that reading, two hours every night, through stacks of library books piled beside her special armchair. This time I was too angry to be impressed.

'I couldn't give a damn who she was.'

'Alex, I'm *sorry*,' said Dad. 'But from the women's page . . . Next time you'll have to be more careful.'

'She might have said Amazonian. They were female warriors,' said Mum. I glared at her.

'She makes me sound like some sort of freak.' I read on. It got worse and worse. ' "Usually talkative and forthright in her opinions, Miss Archer was uncharacteristically tight-lipped when asked about her rival Maggie Benton. 'I'd rather not say anything about Maggie. We can't both go to the Games, that's all.' " That makes me sound as though I don't like Maggie, like we have some sort of feud, but I do like her, even if I can't stand her bloody mother, and that's just not fair.' I looked down at the table so that Dad wouldn't see that my red-rimmed eyes were now brimming over with tears as well as pool water.

'Well. A subtle hatchet job,' said Dad. 'At least there's an implied compliment. All that space, more than Maggie if it comes to that. The lady might not approve of you, but at least she finds you and your family environment interesting. Laugh it off.'

'Laugh it off! I'll be the laughing stock of the school today. And there won't be a next time. Thanks,

Mum,' I added, as she handed me a neatly-wrapped lunch.

'Your friends will know it for the artificial nonsense it is,' she said quietly. 'Most of them probably won't even have read it. Allow yourself to be amused, Alex. It's not important.'

'It's important to *me*. This . . . this *rubbish* . . . That's *me* she's talking about.' And I stomped out of the room and ended up seething on my bed. I thought I had become thick-skinned, but I did not relish the thought of walking into the cloakroom at school, and worse, into morning assembly. It's not that I'm completely green at seeing my name in print. I've had to get used to things being written about me, sometimes by male sports journalists who normally cover rugby or rowing and think swimming is a kid's sport. Even with the regular swimming reporters, it hasn't always been flattering, when I've had bad patches and Maggie's had the upper hand—'MISS ARCHER BEATEN AGAIN', 'DISAPPOINTING SWIM', 'ALEX ARCHER DISAPPOINTS'. There have been predictions that Maggie will win this or that race, loads of stuff about the golden girl Maggie and a steadily diminishing few paragraphs about disappointing old me.

Mum was, as usual, right. Most of my friends had not read the paper; those who had, thought it was a hoot. The few staff who mentioned it were scathing. 'That hypocritical nonsense in the paper this morning. Not one bit like you, Alex,' said the Head as we walked together along the corridor to History class. Coming from her, this was indeed a small victory from shame.

'It wasn't me, Miss Gillies,' I said. 'The interviewer did nearly all the talking.'

'And then put it all into your mouth?'

'Yes.'

'A common distortion. Journalists with preconceived ideas, hearing what they want to hear, and inventing the rest. It was a remarkably shallow piece of writing, wasn't it, especially given your considerable difficulties last year. But tell me, do your male friends quote "seem rather scared of you", unquote? Your friend Andy, did he, even a little?'

She had stopped in a patch of sun, just outside the classroom door. A long row of school photographs, teams of this and that, stared at me as I got my thoughts together.

'Andy . . . didn't, no, not at all. The others . . . well, I train mostly with boys, just boys in our squad. I've had lots of trips away with teams. Andy I'd known for about five years before we, before . . . If I wanted to talk to him, I rang him up. Why not? Life's too short to wait for the phone to ring or some boy to decide he wants to take you out.'

On the rare occasions when Miss Constantia Gillies smiled down from her full six feet two and a half inches, it was as if a lighthouse beamed at you. I got the full treatment.

'Alex, you remind me of the wild gels of my university days in England, in the twenties. They waited for nobody, least of all men. Today, we seem to have gone backwards. There's far too much emphasis placed on the skills of self-adornment, and "home-making", whatever that means, and flirtation.'

12

'I'm no good at flirting.'

'I can imagine. Neither was I.' Her black gown, about twice as long as any other teacher's in the school, created quite a draught as she swept into the classroom. Before the chatter and scraping of chair legs died away as the class stood, she added cryptically, 'But I was *wonderfully* tall.'

Tallness. I suppose there's such a word. 'The tallness of her,' Gran used to say when I began to grow and kept on ever upwards. 'You poor child' was another sigh, until one day I couldn't stand it any longer and sat Gran in a chair and told her firmly that I liked being tall. She got the message.

Once, it was my shortness and fatness that worried Gran. When I went to my first swimming lesson, it was a round little nine-year-old body that lined up shivering with five others on the side of the pool, my black woollen swimsuit already hanging half-way down my thighs.

Dad had decided that I should be taught to swim. The logical place was the outdoor Olympic Pool, only a two-section tram ride distant from our house. My teacher, and later coach and friend, can remember that first time very well, as he once told a reporter. 'She floated high like a dead fish and within two lessons was going like a Bondi tram. She learnt the breathing technique in one lesson. Some kids take two seasons. She had long arms, even longer legs, a resting pulse around fifty and the urge to win: champion material if I ever saw it. She always had to be first and furtherest out from the side of the pool. She was a pain in the neck in that class, so I moved her in with a lot of twelve-year-olds.'

I spent most of those summer holidays at the pool, romping, diving, jumping, swimming for hours on end after my lesson. Mum would bring James and Debbie (Robert wasn't born then) and set herself up with book and picnic basket on the terraces above the pool. I saw older kids training, up and down, up and down. Soon I could do several lengths without stopping, hoping that Mr Jack, a portly and seemingly permanent fixture in baggy shorts, panama hat and grey plastic mac by the side of the pool, noticed me. If he did, nothing was said until the start of the following summer, when I had had my first two lessons in a class of twelve-year-olds. On the way home in the car, Dad asked me if I'd like to go in a race at an inter-club meeting at the indoor pool in town. Mr Jack thought I'd go like a bomb.

It was not a good start. Actually, it was a disaster. Dad virtually had to haul me bodily into the building, I was so nervous. They spelt my name wrongly in the programme. Surrounded by kids in track suits who all seemed to know each other, I nearly froze to death waiting for my race, wrapped only in a towel. I upset the starter by insisting on diving from the side of the pool rather than from the starting-block. The dive itself was a belly flop. When I finally got going, it was straight into the lane ropes. The water was a thick warm soup of salt and chlorine that stung my eyes. But I untangled myself, and set off again, eyes shut, cheeks aflame, and swam so fast through the

14

wash that I overtook the other seven in the race three feet from the finish and forgot to stop.

They allowed me and Dad home from hospital sometime after midnight. The X-rays showed nothing broken. The hand which had hit the wall at ninety miles an hour was the worst bruised, but I had a good purple egg on my forehead, too. At impact, the pain had been so intense that I must have blacked out for a bit and sunk like a stone. My disappearance from view was long enough to cause two stout female officials to leap into the pool fully dressed, and apparently very nearly banging themselves together like a pair of cymbals as they jumped. By this time I was on my way back up towards air. The middle-aged mermaids landed on top of me, stockinged legs and white knife-pleated skirts thrashing around like demented jellyfish. I got hauled to the top. Or maybe we hauled each other.

Dad took charge then, and Mr Jack, and an ambulance person with a black peaked cap and a bag, who felt my pulse and put my arm in a sling in case it was broken. Towels, clothes, and our pale blue Morris Oxford car appeared from nowhere. I remember a nearby official's comment: 'Silly kid, but did you see her *go*! I've never seen such acceleration.' I remember, too, the baleful looks of my two rescuers, permed hair afrizz, peeling off their heavy wet blazers, and shaking the water from their stop-watches. Through the hum of excitement around the crowded pool came a snigger or two. Make the most of it, I flung silently at them as I was carried out, this is my first and last appearance here. Not until Mum pulled the sheet over my slinged-up arm and turned out the light did I allow myself a tear.

Embarrassment was not an unfamiliar sensation, even then. Something about me always seemed to invite attention: I found myself chosen to be leader of this or that, the class captain, giver of the morning talk, organizer of this team, thanker of that speaker, Alex'll do it, she won't mind. Did they think I had no nerves at all? I seem to be incapable of blending in with the landscape, even less with a crowd.

It's not just my tallness. I only have to look in a mirror to see that mine is not an especially pretty face, with my father's rather large nose, and a pointy chin. There is nothing special about my hair, which is short and wispy and what Gran's magazines call dark blonde (read: mouse). I am, however, regarded as photogenic. 'Big smile' call photographers, not easy when I've just lost another race to Maggie. Or there's this obsession with legs, pin-up stuff like World War Two calendars. As I've got older and my legs longer, I've refused to stand propped against pool ladders with one leg bent like Betty Grable.

I suppose I did—and do—talk more than most, and my voice, unhappily at times, seems to carry; but aged nine I was no taller than most of my class mates. The tallness came later. In my first few years in ballet class I was even considered a 'short leg'.

Not long before that fiasco at the pool, there had been another, my first appearance on stage; also my last, I swore at the time. I was supposed to lead a troupe of Daisies on stage for our dance in my ballet teacher's annual concert. It was very grand. A proper theatre was hired, with a great swishing curtain. Our mothers had to make costumes, and we had proper stage make-up. The seniors pranced around in tutus. Only the tinkling piano and scratchy record-player set up in the orchestra pit spoiled the illusion.

Things began badly, first when Mum made it clear the whole family was coming. Dad was going to run me to the theatre an hour earlier, but by the time he'd discovered a puncture and changed the wheel on the car, I got there with only ten minutes to spare to find Miss de Latour nearly beside herself, and punctures no excuse at all.

What happened was hardly my fault. It wasn't that the person working the record-player got the wrong record, only that he put the needle down about a quarter of the way through, and with unbelievable ill luck, right at the point where the first theme was repeated. Of course, I would never have started had I heard strange music from the pit. I skipped confidently out; after a few bars I realized that we were well out of phase with the music.

A real pro, as Miss de Latour told me later, would have gone on regardless. We would, she said, have finished the dance well after the music had finished. The father working the record-player might have been able to give us some more music. It would have been messy, but the audience, recognizing adult bungling, would have forgiven us. It was clearly going to take her a while to forgive me taking the law into my own hands. I had stopped in mid-*pas-de-chat*, put hands on hips, and not once, but twice said to the man below in the orchestra pit, 'You got the music all wrong. Can we start again?' I nearly brought the house down. At that point Miss de Latour high-heeled her way on to the stage, bundled all the bewildered Daisies off, and made some light-hearted comment to the amused audience. In the dress circle, most of my family were under the seats, except for my darling three-year-old sister, who yelled 'There's Alex, she looks funny,' as I shuffled off.

It was the last straw. Second time around, the dance went OK, but I was sick of the whole thing. Curtseying to the applause at the end, I caught a glance from the record-player man. If looks could kill, I'd have gone down like a Dead Swan. I fled from the stage the wrong way, pushed past a flutter of false eyelashes waiting to go on, and in the empty make-up room plastered my face with greasy cold cream and returned my face to normal. I changed into my clothes, crept out the stage door, and into the spare seats at the very back of the dress circle, where I glowered away alone while the senior students did their Little Swans and Bluebirds and the whole of *Peter and the Wolf*. I envied the girl dancing Peter in Russian peasant breeches and cropped hair, she was very nimble with her red boots. One day I'd be Peter: brave, adventurous and famous.

'I loved the Daisies, dear,' Gran said kindly from the front seat of the car. The rest of us, including Mum, were all squashed into the back in layers. 'You danced very nicely.'

I don't want to dance 'nicely', I fumed inwardly,

ignoring the snorts from various quarters. I want to dance like a Bluebird, superbly.

'Mind you,' Gran was going on, 'with those legs, I don't think you'll ever . . .'

'What's wrong with my legs?'

'Too long! Not yet, but look at your parents!'

Sabotaged on all fronts, I can remember thinking, 'I don't want to be tall. I don't want to always have to lead the stupid Daisies or whatever. I want, I want . . .' but I didn't really know what it was I wanted. Except not to have people laugh at me.

My fingertips slice open the water. Briefly I'm an arrow, piercing the blue with every muscle taut, making the most of the thrust from the block.

I dare not trust my mid-flight ears. I think I heard the whistle for a false start. From bitter experience I know I cannot assume anything.

Legs begin to kick. The first strokes, and then with both relief and disgust I'm pulled up short by the rope. It's like a physical blow, rasping roughly across my arms and sending shock waves juddering down to my feet.

Damn and blast! False starts break the spell, break confidence, break rhythm, everything! One often leads to two, and then we're all in dead trouble.

We swim slowly back, trying to get shattered nerves together. Blast and damn you, Maggie; but at least that's one race you're not going to win with a flyer. In the water, a fair fight.

'If there's a break, go with it. Don't waste energy on getting angry.' Mr Jack's last words, among others. 'Use the time in the water to relax. Get out last. Keep them waiting those few seconds. Maggie will be

just as thrown off balance.' So she will; so she is. *Maggie hasn't done a false start in years. She's rattled.*

I look at no one as I haul myself out last, shaking the water off my arms. The starter, immaculate in white, is already waiting to give his pep talk. Already I can feel the coldness seeping through my feet. A sweet man, but get on with it. We line up the second time.

'Take your marks.' We bend down, and then someone does it again.

Maggie stays poised on the brink, so do I. The rest have gone in. Tears of frustration blur my vision. And fear: break on the third time and you're out, Alex, finish, kaput. A humiliating way to let you down, Andy.

The crowd has nearly gone wild. Again the pep talk, though this time we are allowed to get towels and track suit tops for a laughable attempt at staying warm. 'Take it easy, girls. Next one who breaks is out. I'll hold you till every last one is rock steady. There'll be no flyers here.' I look over to where Mr Jack and Dad are sitting, but there is only a blur of faces, eyes, spotlights. This is the event of these nationals, my long-awaited clash with Maggie, the fight to the death. A capacity house, fanfares, overture and beginners please. Reporters' pens dipped in blood. I badly need a pee.

Toes around the block. A dreadful hush. I am cold through and through, literally trembling at the knees, devoid of any thought. I only know that I must not allow myself to break; neither must I be so cautious I *get left behind at the starting post and throw that vital fraction of a second and the race away.*

'Take your marks!'

An intolerable silence. There's not a movement. About five hours pass. My ears are out on stalks.

Bang.

We hit the water as one. This time I notice that the water feels warm, a sure sign of creeping coldness.

We're off to see the Wizard . . .

2

I suppose it was just as well that the first time I was
beaten by Maggie I was already established as Auckland junior champ and record-holder, with brilliant
prospects for the future, or so the papers kept saying.
Otherwise, I might not have put up with playing
second fiddle for so long.

Through three summers I had cut a swathe of firsts
and set more than a few local and national records. I
trained about two and a half miles a day (twice a day
in the long holidays). I wore my first Auckland rep
royal blue blazer and went off singing

My eyes are dim
I cannot see

(not, in our case, from old age, but from badly chlorinated salt water)

I have not brought my specs . . . with . . . ME

in rattly chartered buses with jovial drivers and chaperones to other towns, there to be billeted with
swimming families. I learnt to swim straight, even in
old pools of black, insect-ridden water; wind-swept,
ill-lit, unheated, unhygienic, with cracked concrete

surrounds and slimy wooden changing sheds full of the bugs that gave you athlete's foot.

I learnt what it was to be cold most of the time, waiting in the rain until ten at night for my final race, sodden towel over sodden track suit over sodden swimsuit over goose-pimpled body. I certainly learnt to stop when I came to the end of the pool. In freestyle, no one could touch me. I even won the odd backstroke, butterfly or medley race, putting a few noses out of joint. I learnt how to cope with victory.

The joyride ended one day in August 1956, in the front room, listening with Dad to some fantastic new world records being set over in Queensland, Australia, during the run-up to the Melbourne Olympics. Dawn Fraser was triumphant in the sprint, beating her great rival Lorraine Crapp. Mum, as usual, was in the kitchen, Gran was with her, knitting a sweater for one of us while watching Robbie learning to walk, and the other two were climbing trees outside. Dad turning the knob on the radio was saying quite nonchalantly:

'Four years from now, Alex? Rome?'

I shrugged. I wasn't going to let on I'd just been making that promise to myself. I'd be nearly sixteen, just right if all those amazing Aussies were anything to go by.

Even more carelessly, he continued, 'A little competition wouldn't be a bad thing.'

'What competition?'

'You're hoping to get to the junior nationals this season?'

'Yep.'

'And win a place in the sprint titles?'

'Try,' I lied. I knew from people's times, I had every chance of at least a place. If my times kept improving as they had last summer, I could even beat the fifteen-year-olds. Or so, with all the arrogance of a not-quite twelve-year-old, I thought.

'Mmm. I hear from Mr Jack of a girl who's just arrived from Singapore. New Zealand parents, but she was born there.'

I wasn't actually all that interested, and moved to the piano.

'Name of Maggie. Maggie Benton. She's been swimming in races since she was two.'

'Since *when?*'

'Two, so I'm told. They swim all year round up there, every day. Kids learn to swim before they can walk, literally.'

I slid fluently up and down a B flat major scale, pianissimo.

'I'm told she's very fast. Strong build, not as tall as you, but wiry. Big feet. A worker. Fast.'

Another scale, A major. 'How fast?'

'Times are up to yours.'

A very loud and fast scale this time, A minor. Dad evidently felt he had done his duty, or perhaps he knew when to leave me alone, for I heard the door open. 'You need some competition, Alex, if Rome really is your aim. I think she'll provide it.'

A nonchalant arpeggio or two. 'Good,' I said.

The Olympic Pool opened at the end of October in a northerly gale that went on for days. Several yachts were wrecked in the harbour, and a bitter wind blew me off my bike, but nothing could keep me out of the pool. Under a massive black umbrella and grey plastic mac, doling out the daily half mile stints of this and quarter mile of that, Mr Jack asked me if I'd met the newcomer, Maggie Benton.

'Who's she?' I knew perfectly well. Dad's warning had been niggling.

'Girl from Singapore, might give you a run for your money this season. Didn't your father mention her?'

'Oh, yes, vaguely. Did you say half mile straight, quarter kick, quarter arms only, quarter length sprints, twenty width sprints?'

He nodded. I went. In that wind, it was too cold to stand around, even to glimpse this Maggie Benton. There were only five or six people in the pool battling against the wind and waves, heavy going for the first outdoor swim of the season.

Two or three lengths into the half mile straight, I became aware of a female form, in black racers like me, several lanes away. I was not shaking her off. It was not a feeling I was used to, or that I liked.

At the end of the half mile, I leaned against the wall. It was not easy to see through the driving rain, but I knew talent when I saw it, heading off down the pool again. Easy arms, good rhythm, power. Some people just look right in the water; I know I do, and so did this girl.

Maggie Benton, herself.

We got used to each other, training on opposite sides of the pool, with her coach and his squad over the other side. We said polite hellos and goodbyes, and when we met up in the changing-room talked a bit about school and life in Singapore and where she lived now, but not much more. While maintaining an outward nonchalance, I watched her closely. She was smaller than me, wiry, even stocky, neat in everything, pretty too, in a *Seventeen* model sort of way. She didn't seem to talk much to anyone. Those first few weeks, until we all got some tan, she was even whiter than the rest of us. 'Tropical pallor, but don't let it fool you,' said Mr Jack. Her stroke rate was faster than mine, and I could see she knew what hard work was.

I also noted a stop-watch being expertly wielded by a well-dressed lady, always clacking around the concrete in high heels, obviously her mother. Not discreetly enough, however; Mr Jack had already noticed that she was clocking my time trials. I knew by now that behind his Tweedledum appearance and jolly Aussie teddybear act lay the sharpest pair of eyes and ears around the pool. 'Some nerve!' he said. 'And some joy she'd be having, too. Her length sprints are about point five faster than yours.'

'How do you know?'

He looked around, innocent as Winnie-the-Pooh. 'Ssshh.'

'You've been timing her, too!'

'What me? A sneaky thing like that? Never!' But his eyes were looking past me and I noticed a slight jerk of the hand tucked inside his raincoat. Up the other end of the pool Maggie had just finished a length sprint. 'Never! Besides, the time to crack the whip'll be next week.' After a decent interval, he looked at his stop-watch. 'That, by the way, was thirty-two point one seconds. Not bad for the end of a session. She's consistent.'

I was both dreading and looking forward to our first race. At least, we would both know then where we stood. Maggie had already appeared at a couple of club meetings; Dad had insisted that I give them a miss because I had so much on at school, a Gilbert and Sullivan musical, and other end-of-year and end-of-intermediate-school functions. My absence from the first few meetings and her times had already been noted in the press reports. 'NEW JUNIOR STAR' stated one headline after Maggie's first swim, which to my considerable annoyance happened to be an unofficial Auckland record for the distance as well. I read that 'the first clash between Miss Benton and the current Auckland title and record holder Alex Archer is awaited with great interest', and was noticeably quiet at breakfast that morning.

Maggie won, of course, by point three of a second. Why do I say 'of course'? I had lined up for that first race full of confidence. We exchanged a few words, amiably enough, as we awaited our race, a hundred yards over three lengths. I took note of the greater volume of cheers for me, mostly from our squad mates, when our names were called out.

She won. I led to the first turn, led to the second, and she fought me like a tiger all the way up the last lap. By then I knew I'd gone too fast too soon; knew that my training so far that season wasn't enough to sustain the pace. I was still tired from being Ruth in the three performances earlier that week of *The Pirates of Penzance*, our end-of-year production. This time on stage I'd been in my element, and thrilled to bits when various teachers asked if I'd considered a stage career later on. I had, actually, and rather liked the prospect (after the Rome Olympics). All that leaping around in pirate costume in the second act, brandishing a sword, and projecting the patter song which had taken myself and the two boys most of the year to learn . . .

> *This particularly rapid, unintelligible patter*
> *Isn't generally heard, and if it is it doesn't matter*
> *Matter matter matter matter matter . . .*

It was a good end to my two years at intermediate school.

But stage performances and swimming races don't mix. In the final yards of the race against Maggie I died. The announcer confirmed my fears. True, we'd both broken the Auckland record in the process, but that was little comfort.

We went to our first national championships together in February of 1957. Auckland's brilliant juniors, they called us, future senior champs, future Olympic Games team members with prospects for Rome. Reporters relished this rivalry. We got used to them hanging around, wanting quotes from us or our coaches. We were used to our frequent races during the season, used to each other. Or rather I got used to being second most of the time and to Mrs Benton's sickly smiles sweeping around the pool when Maggie won.

At the championships Maggie made a clean sweep, but I made her work for it. Less than half a second in the quarter-mile, point three in the two hundred and twenty yards, point one in the sprint. The crowds were enthusiastic, the Press likewise. Our clashes became headline news. Returning to Auckland, I turned the tables with one glorious one hundred and ten yards win in March, and further redeemed myself by setting a new national junior record to boot. Mrs Harold Benton did not smile at all that night.

Strange things happened to my body that third form year. I was twelve, so I will not bore you with the usual things that happen to twelve-year-old girls. Unlike my schoolmates who talked behind the bike sheds, I'd always known about babies and periods and wet dreams and French letters and things, which proved Mum (who'd been a nurse and could talk about such things) had done a better job than most. Fortunately, my periods soon settled into a regular routine, hardly noted from month to month except that on those days I took care not to hang around in my swimming togs. Maggie was rather less fortunate —some months she got such bad cramps that she had to take a couple of days off training.

And we both got rosebuds. Again I was glad that my Mum, unlike most, did not immediately whisk me off to a shop for my first bra. Lots of mothers could hardly wait to get their daughters all harnessed up, my friend Julia's for one, and Mrs Benton. Mum waited until I asked, the last girl in the class. I hated the loss of freedom. I went braless around the house, and even my togs, those awful limp cotton things we wore then, became something I enjoyed wearing. At the pool, in the water, I could be free.

*   *   *

I grew in all directions that winter. Soon I was nearly as tall as Mum, which is saying something because she is five feet ten and a half inches. Part of me rather hoped that I might equal her, which I never quite did; a sad part of me knew that I had grown past the point of no return for ballet, or even the stage as a career.

By the start of the next season, I was a strapping five foot seven and still growing and I'd decided if I couldn't play the part of Portia I was going to be a lawyer.

We had another baby in the house. Debbie had just gone off to school and along came another boy, christened Robert Albert after my long-dead grandfather. Mum smiled serenely from the chair where she seemed to spend most of her time plugged in to the baby. Gran washed nappies and cooked and mended and ironed and gardened and fed her hens. Dad worked long hours to get extra overtime pay, and helped with the shopping. For the rest of us, life went on as usual. If it sounds a bit mean to say I wasn't much affected by a new baby brother, that's the way it was. Naturally I was pleased, but I'd been through the baby bit twice before, and there was never any suggestion that Robbie's arrival should have any effect on my routine. Life went on; there were always clean pressed clothes and big meat pies, roasts, lemon custard puddings, and muffins or cheese scones when we got home from school.

It was Gran I worried about, and Mum did too,

but nothing anyone said made the slightest difference. When she wasn't working away at the sink or ironing board, or pegging out clothes, Gran was in her little bedroom, which had become a tiny factory, producing beautiful baby dresses, pink and white, occasionally pale lemon, with elaborate smocking, the sort Royal babies are photographed in. Not for Robbie, obviously, but to sell in a very exclusive baby shop in town.

Sometimes I helped her with the more boring jobs like turning the sashes right side out and sewing on the delicate mother-of-pearl buttons which went down the back. She made them in batches of about twenty at a time. I thought it was a pretty hard way to earn money, but she seemed happy enough. When I asked her once who got the money between what she got for each dress and what I knew they cost in the shop, she simply didn't hear the question. I also wanted to ask what she did with the money she did earn, because she certainly didn't spend it on herself, but the look in her eyes warned me off. A long time later, I found out. We were two of a kind, Gran and me.

Next summer, Christmas of '57, came and went, more of the same. Maggie won all the national junior titles going, set records in every event, and narrowly missed selection for the Empire Games in Cardiff. I was an honourable second. How I pushed her to all those records!

And again, at the very end of the summer, I got everything right just once. I needed that sprint record badly. I'd been seriously thinking of retiring gracefully, and telling Mr Jack I'd had enough. It wouldn't be easy, I was his star pupil, his first real champ. I'd be failing him, too. The papers were generous: 'After a season of pushing Maggie Benton to one title and one record after another, Alex Archer hit form with a brilliant sprint performance at the Olympic Pool last night. She trailed her great rival at the half-way mark, but fought back splendidly to win by a fraction in record-breaking time, confirming that her potential for Rome is virtually as good as that of Miss Benton.'

'Just shows what you can do after four months' solid training,' said Mr Jack. 'Give me a year of your life, and the sky's the limit.'

But how could I, even for Rome? I was too busy. That year, 1958, I got an Honours pass in my piano exam, and although I knew that I could never be a professional dancer, I still loved my lessons and flew through the exam. I got involved in the junior musical production, which was a very boring version of *The Emperor and the Nightingale* especially written for schools, with fake oriental music and slanty eyebrows. I shuffled around as a courtier, singing a solo and saying my few lines through a long drooping moustache that fell off on the first night in the middle of my song and temporarily put the chorus out of action with the giggles.

In the winter term I played hockey in the school Junior First Eleven team. School exams were a pain, but I got respectable marks with a minimum of work. The days were so packed, I hardly saw the family.

Through the winter, Dad took me to training at five thirty am (my first winter training, with the eye problems that went with it). I ate breakfast after the rest of the family, got home from school/lesson/rehearsal just in time to have a meal, then disappeared for homework, or piano practice. Weekends were almost as bad, though I occasionally escaped from Jamie and Debbie squabbling and Robbie throwing three-year-old tantrums and went out to help Gran with her baby dresses. I was as happy as a sandboy, and riding for a fall.

There's my story up to the end of 1958. I'm fourteen years and one month old, five foot ten and one-quarter inches, about to go into the Fifth Form to sit School Certificate, which I don't expect to fail. I'm a 'brilliant prospect' for Rome, a talented stage performer and musician, and I've a reputation for saying what I think. I'm popular in the swimming crowd. I train with the boys because they make me go faster. I don't have time for 'normal feminine pursuits' like dating, or buying clothes or records. Besides, with all my lessons/petrol/pool entrance money/track suits/trips away, and three other children coming up behind, there's no money to spare for Elvis the Pelvis. I've a working relationship with Maggie, but don't ask me what I think of her mother. I hate coming second, though I've had plenty of practice at it.

Can I have 1959 again?

Warm water, glaring underwater lights, and the black shark that is Maggie right alongside me. Surprisingly, my arms feel good, rhythm feels good, at one with the water. It's not always so, especially after false starts; five seconds into a race your chest can be tight, arms sluggish and legs like lead. Then it's hard going all the way, fighting the water, fighting pain and anger.

Anger. Now there's an interesting sort of fuel. After the events of today, I'm fairly loaded with it, and taking off like a rocket. Ten yards down and still I've not taken a breath.

We're spread out in a line across the pool. Soon, about a third of the way down, one head will be seen by the crowd to be marginally in front, the point of the arrow. It must be me. But beware, not only Maggie, but the complete outsider who could beat us both to the turn and then hang on like grim death. Unlikely, but not impossible. In sprints, settled in hundredths of a second, stranger things have happened.

People ask me what I think about when I'm swimming. Right now I hate everyone. I hate Maggie and

35

what she might yet snatch from my grasp, and even more I hate adults who jump to conclusions and spread untrue gossip.

First round is to me. On this lap, where the water is smooth, I can see Maggie's white bathing cap cruising along when I take my first breaths. Hey, Andy . . . I'm about a hand's breadth in front.

There's a long way to go yet, Alex.

3

MEMO TO MYSELF. AIMS FOR 1959.
- *Become national sprint champion. You* can. *It just means beating Maggie.*
- *Pass my Grade seven piano, ballet exam, School Cert.*
- *Get in the First Eleven hockey team.*
- *Shut my big mouth. Be nicer to the brats.*
- *Look after Gran.*
- *Stop growing. I'm tall enough.*

Signed: Alexandra Beatrice Archer
1 January, 1959

Enough for one year. I folded the page carefully, buried it under my mattress, and mused. Even as I wrote that summer morning, with the sun streaming in the window on to my hair (only just dry from training, and acquiring a distinctly greenish tinge from chlorine), I felt weighted down, not with all my goals, but with something else, something new I couldn't define. It wasn't just the previous late night, a New Year's Eve barbecue at one of my swimming friends. I had the feeling that I wouldn't want to know what a crystal ball might tell me about the year ahead.

We'd had a pep talk at the end of the year about

choosing our exam subjects and 'setting yourself realistic goals'. Who'd said that? Not The Gillies, for sure. No, it was Nipples, Miss Hunt, who wore tweed suits with very skimpy sheer blouses, took English and was supposedly the 'Vocational Guidance Counsellor'. 'You must decide, girls. Do you want to strive towards degrees, diplomas, achievements, to be a *career girl?* Or the greater and more realistic satisfaction of motherhood and family?'

Realistic? To win a national title at fifteen? Plenty of Aussies had, Ilse Konrads for one. To be an Olympic rep? There was a team going, someone had to be lucky. To want to do law, to do something challenging? I knew two boys from the school where Andy went who wanted to be lawyers. Why not me? To do something worthwhile with my life, earn more money and have less worries than Dad does? Why not? A husband, children, a nice house somewhere, maybe I could have those as well.

Why did our teachers tell us how marvellous it was being a good wife and mother, when they themselves were not? Did that mean they considered themselves failures? But some of them had pretty interesting lives: for their holidays they travelled overseas, went climbing, tramping, skiing, wrote books. It didn't make sense.

We'd all been asked what we wanted to do when we left school. Many of us would be fifteen soon, said Nipples, and would be assessing how many more years of schooling remained. It was to be hoped that we would all want to try at least for our School Certificate, an important qualification for the jobs open to girls. Some would go on to University Entrance, one or two might even want to try for a university scholarship in their Upper Sixth Form year. She made a scholarship sound both dull and unattainable.

We had all sorts in our class. Sober sorts like me; dizzy sorts who hung around milk bars after school, with or without bright red lipstick; tough types with stained tunics and pony-tails, serving time until their fifteenth birthday when we wouldn't see them for smoke; several who were in with the private school set and spent their entire August holidays skiing and their May ones going to private dances (the record was twenty-two invitations for two weeks of holidays, but then she was both stunning of face and reputedly 'fast').

In response to Nipples' bored voice reading out the class list, we all mumbled our ambitions, some truthfully, some not. A few said they might end up working in a shop, or a factory as a machinist or packer or something. The usual replies were training college, nursing, secretarial college, home science, and then travel. One said journalism, two or three arts degrees, one fine arts. I said law, but I was the only one who did.

Even my close friend Julia, who I'd known since we started primary school together and wanted to be a doctor more than anything in the world, said nursing. 'Why did you say that?' I demanded after class. 'You don't want to be just a *nurse.*'

'Nothing wrong with nursing.'

'No, but . . . you come top in maths, chemistry, biology, Latin, the lot. Anyone can be a nurse.'

'Maybe.' She refused all further discussion on the subject, until she came around a few days before Christmas to bring me a present. Her father, she told me wheezily, had insisted that he couldn't afford to put two sons through university *and* a daughter through medical school. Naturally it was more important that James and Charles, etcetera. Besides, she was his most precious only daughter and he didn't approve of women doctors. 'That's rot,' I said. Her brothers were both creeps, and were going to be creepy things like accountants and stockbrokers. 'And you just took that as gospel?' I asked.

'Mum agreed with him,' said Julia. 'She said she couldn't bear the idea of me going away to Dunedin for six years to cut up bodies. She just wants to keep me at home, or at least in Auckland. And then Dad trotted out my asthma. I'd not be strong enough for years of swot and stress, dissecting rooms and lab work and operating theatres, and wards full of cancer patients and loonies and neurotic women and dying children. That's what he said, his words.'

'But nursing's just as hard, harder in some ways. Mum has always said it's the nurses who take the real brunt. Front line troops and all that.'

'Try telling that to my parents. What I haven't told them or even you yet, is that I want to do obstetrics, deliver babies, do research into methods of childbirth. I know they would say, I'll never get a night's sleep.' She shrugged, bitterly, wheezily, looking lost, the shadows under her eyes darker than usual and

40

her jawline puffy. The more I heard about other peoples' parents the more perplexing it all was. Julia might have been asthmatic, but it wasn't as bad now as when she was in primary school and there was no doubt about her brain, she'd won every science prize going as long as I could remember. I hugged her and wiped away her tears and rubbed the knobbles up and down her thin back until the wheezing noise had quietened down a bit. 'Julia, don't lower your sights.'

'There's been the most almighty row already. Dad shouting and telling me how cruel I am, upsetting Mum like that, can't I see all she wants is my happiness.'

'You've got two years yet. It won't make any difference to what subjects you do for School C, will it? I don't know why you told them so soon.'

'It just slipped out. We had a sort of uncle visiting from Australia, a second cousin of Mum's, something high up in insurance on transfer back here for a year. Somehow I told him, and it came out at the dinner table, you know . . . I suppose he thought they might be proud of me, or something . . .'

'Well, they might learn to be.'

'Not my father. He'll use my asthma . . .'

'Haven't the doctors always said you'll grow out of it? And aren't there all sorts of new drugs coming through? There'll be a way,' I said, but without total conviction. Her father was a factory manager, a tough nut to crack.

'I'm sorry, but it's nice of you to ask me.'

'Miss Archer, I don't think you understand,' said

the man calling long-distance from somewhere near Wellington. 'Our new pool is the best in the North Island. This Gala Opening is the climax of three years' fund-raising. We've lined up water ballet, diving, gymnastics, bands, marching girls, a carnival queen contest, even a rock 'n' roll group. Our Member of Parliament will be there, and the Mayor and . . .'

'If you've got all that, you don't need me.'

'Oh yes . . .'

'It's only four days before the nationals. I'd have to taper off my training a week earlier, and I haven't got that sort of time.'

'We're relying on you and Miss Benton. A Grand Invitation one hundred and ten yards, climax of the evening, sneak preview to the championships. In country areas like this, our people seldom get the chance to see a duel between two such great rivals.'

'Is Maggie coming?'

'Yes, she accepted immediately. Actually, we were hoping that you might come down together.'

Not on your nellie. With her mother? 'I can't.' Disconcerted by his persistence, I added, unwisely, 'Put her against the boys.'

A horrified silence. 'Boys? Girls don't swim against boys.'

'I'm joking, Mr . . . Sorry I didn't hear what your name was. I'm known for my funny sense of humour.'

'My name is Cleverly. Well, naturally, we'd pay your airfare, and my wife and I would be delighted . . .'

'I can't race Maggie four days before the nationals.

I'll just be getting over the Auckland champs, which everyone says she's going to win anyway. I'm sorry.'

He tried a last tack. 'We've already had the posters printed.'

Oh, help. I wavered. Perhaps I *could* go straight from there to the nationals in Wellington. Who with, and how, and where did I stay when I got there? It would only work if Dad was prepared to come with me, and he was in the middle of his two weeks' annual leave right now and he'd never before been able to get any extra time off, even when Mum had babies. But surely the poster was Mr Cleverly's problem, not mine. He should have asked sooner.

He sensed my hesitation. 'Couldn't you come down with Miss Benton and go straight on to your championships? Or fly down and we'll fly you home the next day? It's just one event, one exhibition race . . . ?'

With Maggie it was never just that, and especially now. 'I'm sorry. These nationals are too important to me . . .'

'To give something back to the sport that supports you?'

'That's not . . .' very fair, I was saying, to myself.

'I'd like to speak to your coach, if you don't mind. Can I ring him at the pool?'

Did I have any choice? 'Yes, any time. He's the assistant manager there,' I said wearily. Three weeks to the nationals. Training was a twice daily ordeal and time trials a nightmare. I was having sunburn problems, and sinus problems, and rash problems with my swimming togs. Maggie's time trials were getting better and better. The Auckland champs next week were going to be a Maggie Benton benefit, I knew already. I didn't need some smooth-talking organizer on my back as well.

'I'll ring him right away,' he said, adding, 'perhaps I should have rung him first.' And the line went dead. I went to find Dad in the garden. 'Unfortunate timing,' he grunted, in between swipes at the hedge with a nasty-looking sickle. 'A hard decision for you, but I've no doubt the right one. These people . . . how do you get through to them?' He paused, maybe to emphasize his next words. 'Be prepared for some flak.'

'The right decision, Alex,' said Mr Jack when I saw him at the pool later in the day. 'I had to tell that persistent fellow to stop putting the acid on. You don't race to order, mine or anyone else's. He should, of course, have gone through the proper channels first, rather than coming to you direct. But the result would've been the same. Be prepared for some flak.'

'That's what Dad said.'

'I mean real flak. Our friend's taking it higher. Centre officials and Press. Pressure will be exerted. You'll be accused of bad sportsmanship, among other things.'

Across the pool, Maggie was resting between time trials and getting an earful from her mother, who was using her stop-watch quite openly now and writing my times down in a little book.

'I *can't* go.'

'Agreed. I'll support you. I'll talk to any Press who come stirring. You, my girl,' he poked a stubby

44

finger, 'would be advised to say nothing.' Behind the genial smile, the warning was clear. 'Now, half mile straight, two quarters time trial, four two hundred and twenties . . .'

And a thousand length sprints, I thought wearily, as I looked down the pool for a free lane and patted down the large piece of sticking plaster under my arm which covered a patch of raw skin, the chafing of tens of miles. Why do I do it?

That was a question I asked myself more than once in the next few weeks as I pushed Maggie to new junior records in all the Auckland champs, and we both put in some long hard grind in preparation for the nationals. The rest of the country was on holiday, sporting in the sun.

The flak from my refusal to race against Maggie in the Manawatu gala had been short, 'a storm in a teacup', as Mum said mildly, but some sharp things were said by various officials in the papers. Mr Jack did his bit to defend me but it all read as though I was a spoilt brat. A centre official, upright in navy blazer and indignation, arrived during training one night and kept Mr Jack in the office and us waiting for nearly half an hour. 'Sorry about that, team' was all he'd say when he returned to finish our time trials. 'Keep smiling, Alex,' he added when we'd mercifully finished, and Andy and I were sitting gasping on the side of the pool. 'Interesting, really. You need officials to run the races, just like they need swimmers to compete. But it's not the officials who get up at five in the morning, day in, day out, and they need to be reminded of that, occasionally. The problem comes when money starts talking. It seems those people have spent a fair whack on their pool opening. You were the only thing money couldn't buy. My God, Alex, that man Cleverly didn't offer you any, did he?'

'No, course not.'

He whistled, a long tired phew of relief. There was more to being a coach than just standing on the side of the pool dishing out schedules. Mr Jack absorbed all my worries like a big comfortable sponge.

'Do you think I should go?'

'No. But next time don't talk to these people, officials, organizers, what-not. Put them on to me, straight off. That's what I'm here for.'

One night I found myself in the changing sheds with Maggie. It may have been deliberate; generally we preferred to change at different times. She had parked her English dress and the beautiful American petticoat which made the dress stick out like a lampshade unusually near my limper version and Gran-made sun-dress. As we dried and dressed, we exchanged pleasantries, but this day there was more. She was a neat girl, was Maggie, controlled in everything she did, but she seemed to be taking her time rolling up her towels. Finally, she said, 'I'm sorry you're not coming to that thing in Manawatu next week. You could've come in the car with us, and then on to Wellington.'

'Oh, well, you know why. It's been splashed about the papers enough,' I said ungraciously.

She dried her dark curls in front of the mirror, carefully arranging the fringe and side bits in kiss-curls like Audrey Hepburn. 'I hate long car trips. It would've . . .'

She dried up. I looked at her sharply from under my own spiky hair. Would've what? Been nice, been fun? Perhaps, with only a much younger sister, she would've actually enjoyed my company, any company, deflecting for a while the unrelenting beam of her mother's attention. 'It's even longer in the bus.'

'Yes, but there's lots of singing. And getting out to buy fish 'n' chips and fizzy drink, things I'm never allowed 'cause Mother thinks they're bad for me. And games and . . .'

I looked at her even more curiously. Come to think of it, Maggie only rarely went on the bus trips. Usually her mother took her in their great big Austin car. 'You sound like you don't much want to go yourself. They'll make a big fuss of you. Queens in white kid gloves and the Member of Parliament. Bands and marching girls. Lovely.'

She pulled a face at the mirror. 'A lot of pompous speeches, and strange people. And fuss. I hate fuss.'

She did? I had always thought she coped with fuss remarkably well, always pleasant to reporters, obliging to photographers, polite to officials; unlike me, who was known to have been terse with all three. 'Then why did you say you'd go, straight off, the man said.'

'It wasn't straight off. We talked about it first, then we rang Mr Upjohn and he accepted for us. Mum thought I should.'

'The lying hound! That man, I mean,' I added hastily. So she'd done everything right, been through all the proper channels. 'And I suppose she thought I should, too.'

'Yes, um, no, I mean . . .'

'She said as much in the paper.'

'That's only her. In your position I'd have done the same.'

In *my* position? But there was no irony in her voice, no sideways smile, nothing to suggest she was playing games with me. She meant just what she said. I relented a bit.

'You'll enjoy it when you get there. They're good kind people really, if you don't include that Mr Clever Dick. Three years raising money, it's a big thing for them.' It wasn't original: Mum's contribution, actually, to our family discussion on whether I should have gone. (Verdict: Not guilty.)

'I suppose so. Still, I wish you were . . . well, see you.' As she zipped up her bag and left abruptly it occurred to me for the first time that Miss Maggie Benton, Olympic prospect, soon to be *Weekly News* cover girl and darling of the Press, could actually be rather lonely.

Well, Maggie went off to be the star turn at the opening, while I trained like a mad thing during the final run-up to the nationals: thousands of sprints and starts and turns. Fat lot of good it did me. Maggie, rested, cheerful and confident, was already in Wellington when we arrived after a dreadful bus trip that took over twelve hours. Half the team sick, and the bus getting slower and slower, finally grinding to a halt. Electrical problems or something. By the time we arrived, we were all dying of hunger, or boredom; or frantically trying to sleep.

It was a rotten start to the week, too. The champs were at a new pool, but four events and two relays were more than enough, with heats and finals morning and evening. Sure, I had the minor satisfaction of edging out two former rivals in my best times ever, and Mr Jack was full of theories that this was exactly what he wanted in the two-year run-up to Rome. And, again, the wiser reporters said nice things about me as well, but it was Maggie who climbed to the top of the victory dais.

After the nationals it was straight back to school, where I was treated (just for a morning) as a returning hero rather than the 'also-ran' that I thought I was. Four silvers in national senior titles were enough to warrant special mention at assembly, with La Constantia in full flight, burbling on at great length about individual achievement and all-around ability and hauling me up on the stage to be gawked at by seven hundred pairs of eyes.

'A credit to the school, Alex. Well done and good luck,' she finished. Hearty round of applause from the serried ranks of black gym tunics while I shuffled about in front of the senior teachers lining the stage like a row of smiling black cats, all smug and comfortable.

Had I but known, it was not to be long before the claws came out, mine as much as anyone's. Soon

America would shoot two monkeys into space, the Chinese would march into Tibet, and Aucklanders would queue to see Dame Margot Fonteyn dance *Giselle* with the Royal Ballet and/or hear Billy Graham. In the same month, the Auckland harbour bridge would open for business, I would go to my first dance and someone would whisper that Alex Archer was really rather a mannish sort of girl with her broad shoulders and flat chest and slim hips and long legs, always hugging other girls after her races—and nothing would ever be quite the same again.

Concentrate!

One hand has brushed the corks that make up the lane ropes. That might cost me a hundredth of a second, and the race. Can't you swim straight, even now, just once, Alex, your last chance?

Concentrate! The turn is coming up. It must be nothing less than perfect. Races and trips have been decided on a single turn.

Into deeper water, darker blue glass. On both sides, through the criss-cross patterns of underwater lights, are bodies hard at work. I'm leading.

And not only by a hand, more an arm's length. What has happened? 'Go out hard,' Mr Jack said. (I've done that.) 'Pile on the pressure.' (That too.) 'You'll need every bit you can get for the return journey, flying blind.'

The turn, idiot! Where are the red lane markers, the black lines on the bottom of the pool, to judge how far? I have a moment of sheer panic that I've missed them and am about to slam into the wall. I'm nine years old again.

I got all three turns right in the two hundred and

twenty yards two days ago. It was one of those races where everything clicked. That, and pushing myself past the pain barrier into a silence where I swear I heard Andy call my name, was why, contrary to all expectations, I won it! The quarter mile on Tuesday had been Maggie's. I had to win the two hundred and twenty to stay in the running. One each, then, and Mrs Benton up to all sorts of mischief. Why can't you just leave Maggie and me alone to slog it out?

This is the decider, here and now, for Rome. May the best woman win, and her mother go to hell.

Despite the false starts, I'm feeling good. I'm flying over the water with that delight in my own speed, my own power, which only comes when everything is right. Make the most of it. The pain, the real work is yet to come.

Five yards to the turn. Right or left arm will touch? Alarm bells ring. Prepare to dive!

Help me, Andy!

4

'Who will you ask?' said Mum, as I stared at the blue frilly-edged card that waited for me after school. Three girls—one of them Maggie Benton—were inviting Miss Alexandra Archer and Partner to a dance to be held at some cabaret I'd never heard of, 20 May, 1959. RSVP by 10 May.

'What did she ask me for?' I said. 'I'm not in her crowd. And she's still fourth form.' It was a small satisfaction to me that she was.

'Don't you want to go?'

'Suppose so.' Translation: No I don't, because I'm scared stiff. Who with, and what do I wear, and how do you foxtrot let alone quickstep! I half-hoped that Mum would tell me, as she always had before, that I was still too young for teenage dances; it was different for Julia or my classmates who were mostly a year older. Mum was, however, saying nothing of the kind. She was off on a tangent of her own.

'Makes me feel quite old.'

'What does?'

'Daughter going to her first dance. Mine was a country hop, I was fifteen and taller than you. All the girls huddling down one side of the hall and the boys down the other, glaring at each other. Kids screaming up and down on the white powder they put down

53

to make the floor slippery. Dads out the back with the beer, mums watching their daughters like hawks.'

'Sounds like nothing has changed,' I said, thinking of a certain mother I knew.

'Ancient band of piano, sax and drums. Awful. And if your partner was the boorish sort, and most were, or you were unusually tall or even if you weren't, he'd sneak out the back for a beer. You'd end up a wallflower. Fate worse than death.'

'Did anyone actually dance?'

'Oh yes, enough. Quite often women together, fed up with sitting around waiting.'

'Mum, I don't think I want to go to Maggie's dance. It sounds too . . . too grand for me.'

'Oh dear, Gran was so looking forward to making your first formal dress.'

'She can do that later. Fifth Form, Sixth Form dance or something. Anyway, who could I ask?'

'Andy, surely? Well, think about it, Alex. I mean that about a dress. And Dad'll teach you to do the foxtrot. With all your ballet, you'll pick it up in two minutes.'

Clever old Mum. And cunning. She'd answered all my worries. Of course I could ask Andy, my swimming and special friend since primary school days, three years older and just a bit taller than me. He was in his last year at school sitting scholarship exams. He'd done all sorts of sports: First Fifteen rugby in the winter, tennis, a bit of water polo, surfing, but mostly swimming and yacht racing. Since we were juniors, we'd trained together during the long summer holidays once exams were over. I chased him on time trials up and down the pool. He usually made the Auckland champs finals; he was my keenest supporter as I progressed towards national level. We'd shared lots of things: books like Homer's *Odyssey* and Kingsley Amis' *Lucky Jim*, radio Goon Show jokes, and music. While most people were falling over Elvis, Ray Charles, Bill Haley and the Comets, Dean Martin, Pat Boone, even Little Richard (serious question: why are all pop stars men?) he introduced me to Noel Coward, Gershwin and Errol Garner, and I introduced him to ballet and musicals. We shared great ambitions. I was the only person in the world who knew what he really wanted to do. His father thought it was medicine, but I knew differently.

I knew Andy could dance, because he'd complained bitterly two or three years before about his father making him learn ballroom dancing. Then he'd actually enjoyed it, and I felt . . . jealous? Still a child, which I suppose I was then.

I decided to go to Maggie's dance when I heard several others in the swimming crowd had also been invited. Andy was happy to oblige. I went shopping with Mum and Gran for material and a pattern. Dad marched me around the living-room and pronounced me a 'quick learner', (to my disgust) 'easy to lead', and I wrote a formal letter in my best handwriting on stiff paper. 'Miss Alexandra Archer thanks Maggie Benton, Susan Clarkson and Tania James for their kind invitation . . .'

Maggie was simply holding out the hand of friendship, I reassured Julia, who seemed to think there was some ulterior motive behind the invitation. I couldn't for the life of me imagine one, and neither could she, when pressed. I hadn't seen Maggie in weeks. The season had fizzled out, and we were taking a break. Training, when it started again at the beginning of the May holidays, would be for real, with heavy distance work, calisthenics and weights.

Not that I was twiddling my thumbs. I had end-of-term tests at school, hard work at my new piano pieces, ballet twice-weekly and rehearsals for *The Wizard of Oz*, the current school show, which somehow I'd auditioned for and ended up in. We'd had the first trials for the hockey teams; I saw myself going straight from Junior to Senior First Eleven, right half.

Maggie's dance, middle weekend of the holidays, loomed. Gran and Mum talked on about their first dances, putting your hair up and stuff on your eyelashes and biting your lips to make them pink; country hops, rugby club socials, church dances and city balls; debutantes, hovering chaperones and men in white gloves and patent leather dancing pumps. It all sounded a long way from waltz and rock 'n' roll at a 1959 teenage dance. The kids, home and fighting fit, didn't let a day go past. Andy, my friend, had suddenly become 'the boyfriend'. Like dogs, they knew their victim.

'What's that for?' Andy, done up in suit, tie, pink carnation but no Brylcreem because he knew I hated the stuff, was holding out a small bunch of flowers.

'You, clot.'

'How did you know I was wearing pink?'

'I asked you last week.'

So he had, a special phone call, for this very reason. I'd been rather rude, demanding why he wanted to know.

'You put it on your left shoulder,' he said.

'I do?' The brats all danced around the hall, jeering, while Andy pinned the silver-wrapped stalk to my dress, and I prayed my breath smelt okay and the Tangee Natural lipstick was on straight and I hadn't overdone the mascara. 'Hey Mum, the boyfriend's brought flowers, oooh,' shouted Robbie, while Jamie did an Elvis: 'A *white* (wiggle of hips) 'sports coat' (another wiggle) 'and a pink carNATion', until Dad appeared to rescue me ('That's enough Jamie,' in the low voice he kept for last warnings) and shake Andy's hand. 'Nice to see a man is punctual.' Mum and Gran leaned against the archway at the other end of the hall, giving me a final once-over. It was a nice dress, coral pink satin cotton, with a boat neckline, wide belt, and full circle skirt. Even with the extra pounds I'd put on in the lay-off from training, it had crossed my mind I could almost pass for something out of *Seventeen*.

But I simply couldn't understand why I, used to standing up in front of crowds of people, was feeling such stage fright. And with Andy! It was ridiculous, although he did look mildly uncomfortable himself.

'Off you go then,' said Dad through the commotion. I sailed grandly through wall-to-wall family, clutching my white nylon stole as the brilliant May night hit my bare arms.

'Chilly,' I said, making for the car door. Andy was quicker and beat me to the handle. 'I can do that.'

'No, let me.'

He'd taken me home from training in his mother's Volkswagen many times. 'You've never opened doors for me before,' I said.

'I've never taken you to a d-d-dance before.' We fell into the car and an uneasy silence. The VW didn't run to a radio.

I've been cherishing—Through the perishing
Winter nights and days—A funny little phrase
That means—Such a lot to me
That you've got to be
With me heart and soul
For on you the whole—Thing leans.

It was easier singing Noel Coward than talking, so I took the cue,

Won't you kindly tell me what you're driving at
What conclusion you're arriving at?

I'd noticed before that, when singing, Andy didn't stutter, even the d words, which were sometimes d-d-a problem before he found another word to use. He sang the answer,

Please don't turn away—Or my dream will stay
Hidden out of sight
Among a lot of might-
Have-beens!

and together we sang the rest of 'A Room with a View' which got us safely to the driveway of the cabaret. Cheerful groups of four and six at a time were getting out of other cars. I'd turned down Andy's offer of going to someone's house 'for drinks' beforehand. I began to fuss with bag and stole and white nylon gloves and skirts.

'Now, Alex Archer. You sit right there.'

'Why? We're going inside, aren't we? Isn't this the place?'

'The rules say a girl waits for the car door to be opened by her escort. Here beginneth the gospel according to Mrs Richmond, chapter one, verses one to t-t-sixty, read to me at great and tedious length before I left. So wait, damn you.'

Andy got out, locked his door, and came around to open mine with an Elizabethan flourish. I stepped out, Marilyn Monroe from her limousine, Audrey Hepburn on a Roman holiday—no, Junoesque Jane Russell was nearer. Who you kidding, lady? Music was already coming from the hall, and figures could be seen moving around inside.

'Now you take my arm,' he said.

'So I don't trip on the stones in my high heels and fall over? Or get raped and pillaged on the way?'

'That's right.'

Our eyes met, and we both broke out laughing.

'This is ridiculous,' I snorted. 'Let's get on with it.'

'Lead on.'

Running the gamut of the reception committee in the foyer was another matter. There was Maggie, lady-like in pale blue taffeta and pearls, her escort a

Brylcreem ad, the other hostesses also desperate to do the right thing in front of their parents. It was a film set: chandeliers, flowers, silk dresses, hairdos, dinner jackets, air thick with perfume, the band playing Glenn Miller. This was a teenage dance! Fourth and Fifth Formers! I caught some stage whispers. 'That's Alex Archer. The swimmer. Big girl, huge,' that sort of thing. Maggie seemed pleased to see us. Mrs Benton was overboard with joy. After a quick once-over lightly of me and partner, her smile was warmth itself, her outstretched hand regally limp. My hands were cold, but hers was colder, a little broomstick of bones.

'Alex dear. How *well* you're looking.' (Translation: You've put on weight.)

'You know Andy Richmond?'

'Yes, of course. I've seen you training with Alex many times, haven't I? You're the young man who's hoping to do medicine. How nice of you both to come.' (Translation: I do my homework. Your partner is approved.)

We were saved by a blast from the band. 'Do go through,' she piped. 'The ladies' cloakroom is over there.' Her eyes were already on the next guests to be given the royal welcome.

Andy, nodding thanks for favours bestowed, took a firm grip on my elbow and steered me down the foyer's green swirled carpet. 'Spare me! Where's her tiara? You go in there,' he muttered, nodding towards a closed door marked Powder Room. 'The holy of holies.'

'The what?'

'The cloakroom. You leave your things in there.'

He knew what I was going through. It wasn't his first dance; he knew it was mine.

Inside there was much swishing of taffeta and plumping up of well-padded bosoms and straightening of stocking seams and reglossing of mouths. I knew not one carefully-prepared face. For the first time in my life I was feeling my tallness, aware of curious stares in the mirror. The family was playing Monopoly at home tonight. I wished I was there.

Andy proved as easy to dance with as Dad. It was odd, being so close to someone, whose body (in swimming togs) I knew so well. I was just beginning to relax when a short gent in tails rushed into the middle of the room, all bonhomie and bright ideas. The snowball and excuse-mes passed as bad dreams, but at least I wasn't left standing, rather the opposite. Grasped by a lanky, acne-ridden youth with a fake English plum accent for the dance where they spun a beer bottle and if it pointed to your corner you were out, I prayed for the bottle to point at me. As the numbers dropped, and the little gent got more and more red in the face, my jitters rose. The waltz rhythm was completely beyond my partner; not that he was aware of it, as he held me rigidly at arm's length and talked about the harbour bridge being opened next week.

'They're having this walk across the bridge. A once-only chance for the proles.'

'Oh really?'

'Are you going?' he asked.

'Ah guess ah might.'

'Are you American?'

'Oh yes, ah come from Milwaukee.' It was the first place that flashed into my mind.

My prayers were finally answered. The bottle pointed and we were out. We slunk to the edges. I couldn't regain control of my hand. Andy, bless him, steered his partner around towards me as the winners were declared.

'How'd ya be?' he muttered.

'Awful.' I didn't know Andy's partner, frolicsome in pale pink polka-dotted frills and remarkably high stilettoes. We all grinned bleakly at each other.

'Sorry,' I said to Plum, 'What d'ya call yourself?'

'Christopher. Christopher Allardyce.'

It would be. I'd had enough, and since Polka-dot's arm was twined up Andy's, I had to escape by myself. I needed some fresh air and a pee, and to extricate my hand from the damp grip of Mr Allardyce.

'Excuse me, I need to visit the bathroom,' I heard myself say. Andy's face was a picture.

'The supper waltz is soon,' said Andy as I disengaged. It was all I could do not to wipe my hand on my dress.

'And?'

'May I have the pleasure?'

'Oh. Yes. Thanks.' Remembering, 'Sure, baby.' I had to cross acres of slippery floor, through couples standing stiffly round waiting for the next dance to begin. One boy seemed to move deliberately into my path, and his hips brushed along mine. 'Not bad, honeybun,' he breathed beerily into my ear. A cheeky hand cupped itself under the curve of my buttock, or would have, given fewer layers of petticoat. Thrown off balance, I went over on the side of one flimsy white sandal. Something gave. It was a strap, broken. I bent down, picked up the shoe and walked with as much dignity as I could summon into the sanctuary of the Ladies, and on into an empty toilet. If the overheated fumes of hairspray, deodorant, perfume and BO didn't knock you out first, there, at least, was privacy.

One strap pulled away and a whole shoe useless! Who designed these things? And who bought them, more fool me. As I stared at the shoe angrily, I heard the outside door swing open.

'Look at my stockings. Ripped to shreds. What a *clod*hopper! I'm going to have blue toes for a week.'

More of the same, two or three of them lamenting certain partners with feet like pile-drivers and girls who waltzed past drawing blood with stiletto heels spiking into unsuspecting ankles. I was beginning to wonder if dances were all they were cracked up to be.

'And I've got a bone to pick with mine, slimy creature. That gorgeous tall girl, the swimmer, I saw him when she went past.'

Uhh?

'You mean Alex Archer? Maggie's swimming pal? What a figure!'

'If you want to be six feet tall and built like a tank.'

'But you watch the boys, the looks she's getting.'

'Little do they know.' Darkly.

'Know what?'

Voice lowered. 'Well, you know.'

'I don't know.'

'Well . . . those great shoulders and slim hips. More like a man if you ask me. I've heard it said . . .' the voice faltered, for maximum effect.

'What?'

'I've a friend at her school who says it's no accident she always winds up being a male in their school plays. Apparently, she's always hugging the girls after races. And she's got this very special friend Julia at school. Imagine Maggie and Alex Archer in the same race. Hardly fair, really. Maggie's half the size.'

I could either wait until they'd gone, or throw a spanner in the works. Ears on fire, I decided I'd heard enough. Taking off the other shoe, I flushed the toilet, rearranged my dress, and stepped grandly out. It was worth it if only to see their faces. Such a rush of blood upwards. One was a proper little dumpling in scarlet lace and black gloves to her armpits, the other all crimpy permed and hung about with diamante. Barefoot, I smiled sweetly at them both before padding over to wash my hands. Within five seconds they'd snapped their clutch bags shut and fled.

My own cheeks were none too pale, either, flushed to a deep mottled purple under the terrible neon lights. From the pile of bags and stoles, I found the little evening bag Mum had lent me, got out a comb and forced myself to look myself in the eye. My hands were shaking. Is *that* what people were saying?

Did they say it of Julia too? Was it peculiar to hug when you wanted to congratulate someone; odd to rub Julia's back when she got wheezy?

The door swung open again to admit another girl-ish gaggle, cackling away. Their shiny faces swum in the mirror, one vaguely familiar from Maggie's swimming squad.

'Hi, Alex. How's things?'

If I ever needed my acting talents, it was now. 'Fine, thanks', I said. In the mirror I saw my gay, brittle smile and glinting eyes, and below them the wide ('great') shoulders I had been rather proud of.

'You cold? You're shaking.'

'Am I?'

'It's the supper dance next. Where're your shoes?'

I pointed to the floor. 'Come apart.'

'You poor thing. What're you going to do? You can't go around in your stockinged feet.'

'Why not?' I snapped, surprised that even she seemed to think it so important. 'Do I have any choice?' I swept past her out into the foyer, where the first person I saw was the faithful Andy, waiting just along from the door. I almost ran at him.

'Where're your shoes?'

'Why are people so obsessed with my shoes? One broke.' He was looking at me closely. 'Well, I didn't do it on purpose, did I? Stupid things. Someone pushed me over.'

'You all right?'

'Of course I'm all right. I'll just have to go barefoot for the rest of the evening, that's all. Do you mind too much? If people want to think it's because I can't bear being tall . . .'

'What's . . . ?

'. . . and I feel an overwhelming desire to be a normal female size, that's their business.' My voice was shrill. I couldn't help it.

'OK, OK. Let's d-d-dance. It's the supper waltz.' I felt a strong arm around my waist; I was being propelled towards the dance floor. I'd been about to ask him to take me home.

'That pill,' he said into my ear, 'what's-his-name, with the English accent . . .'

'Christopher something. What about him?'

'Frightfully put out, when I asked you to supper. He had the same idea, I could see a mile off. Muttered something in his beard and walked off.'

'Tough.' At this range he could see the tears in my eyes. I kept my face well turned to the left.

'You dance well, Alex. Much better than most.'

'Thanks.'

'What's with the Yankee accent? He wanted to know, were you an American F-Field Service scholar.'

'Stow it, Andy.'

I knew I was still shaking, and that Andy was aware of something peculiar going on. Then I saw one of my accusers, she of the tomato-red lace and heavy eyebrows, dancing with the dark fellow who had pushed me over. I glared at them both. Her eyes dropped immediately, he winked and leered. I made sure I was still glaring when she looked over again, with such a smirk on her face that the thought occurred that I might have been meant to overhear what I did, revenge for her boyfriend's finding me baggage worth handling. Cheap. And cruel. And yet— how many other tongues wagged? Why, why?

I put on a good show, with my stockinged feet and breaking heart, receiving curious looks and laughing it gaily off; through asparagus rolls, cheerios on sticks, chocolate log and fruit salad at supper; meeting a lot of people that Andy seemed to know; through the statue dance (I accidentally-on-purpose over-balanced very early on); and the last half hour of rock 'n' roll where, with things loosened up a bit and me past caring, I learnt very quickly how to rock around the clock tonight. Fast footwork and pirouettes were called for, and ballet came in handy. Andy could be forgiven for thinking I was enjoying myself; it was a dance of defiance, with skirts swirling high around my hips, and my long legs bared to stocking-tops and even suspenders for any who cared to look. One who did was Plum, lurking in the entrance with a cigarette drooping from his lips, and a twist to his mouth that said that rock 'n' rolling was beneath him. 'You made a hit there,' murmured Andy. 'Get me away,' I said, and instantly found myself in the thick of the crowd, away from his hungry eyes.

'Straight home?' Andy said, as the balloons came down after 'Auld Lange Syne' and all the little boys chased around popping them in their partners' ears.

I nodded. I'd needed all my stamina to last this long. A last visit to the Ladies to get my things and it would all be over. That was achieved, mercifully, without seeing anyone I knew. Maggie was at the door, saying goodnight. So, unluckily, was her mother. She still looked fresh and grimly gracious, not a permed hair out of place.

'Alex dear, wonderful to watch you dancing barefeet. Quite the belle of the ball.' (Translation: You were conspicuous. It is not done.)

'My shoe broke, Mrs Benton.'

'You must take it back.' (Translation: And get better ones.)

Andy intervened then, with loud thanks to all and sundry for a wonderful dance. I said about two words of thanks and left him to it. Down the steps and (painfully) across the gravel in my stockinged feet, and shortly the crunch of shoes catching up with me.

'That woman is a pain.'

'She also hates my guts. But Maggie's OK.'

'Where was f-f-father amongst that lot?'

'Overseas, on business. He's not around much.'

'Maggie didn't look as though she enjoyed her own d-d-dance much either, poor kid.'

Kid? Did Andy see me as a child, too? I was, after all, only a few months older. Too much had happened too fast. I could think only of getting home, to my own bed. I couldn't open the car door because Andy had to unlock it, a tedious wait in the bitter moonlight, which set me shaking anew. Then there was all the chivalrous bit again, before Andy drove off and there was another uneasy silence.

Couldn't they see that the only reason why I took male roles in school shows was that being at a girls' school someone had to.

And what about our Third Form year and getting swept up in the fashion for declaring your undying love for a certain senior girl? Mine had been Leonie, dark and Spanish-looking, a prefect, promising singer, lead in school shows, captain of tennis, A-team netball, now studying at the School of Music. I would have done anything she asked me. From the great heights of the Fifth Form I now knew this was simply innocent heroine-worship. It was love, of a kind. Everyone knew hero-worship went on at boys' schools, why not at girls'?

I suspected that two of the little thirds currently felt that way about me, nudging each other in corridors and thinking themselves unnoticed when they followed me home from school. But had I smiled at them, would that have set tongues wagging? Had it already? And my own classmates, old friends since primary days—did they edge away from me when I had to be a man in plays, or avoid contact in sardine assemblies, or wonder about the hug when you won a hockey match or holding hands for games? I knew they didn't. It was crazy! I hugged people because I was pleased for them, winning things, or it seemed to help when someone was in tears about something. I rubbed Julia's back at school sometimes because it seemed to help her wheezes. So what?

As we turned into my street, I remembered I'd been dreading the last bit, the kiss in the car or at the front door that was much discussed at school. Maybe Andy didn't even want to. ('Little did they/he know!') But he just sang a sad little song, *The party's over, It's time to turn out the lights*, as he pulled up outside the house, did his final escort duties, and gave me a brotherly hug on the front doorstep. 'Thanks for asking me, Alex. See you Saturday night, around six?'

'Saturday?'

'The Sixth Form dance? We've been asked to Jeff's place beforehand.'

'Oh yes. Thanks.' The thought did not thrill me much.

Mum's reading light was still on. 'Enjoy yourself?' she whispered as I bent to kiss her goodnight and put her book on the cluttered table beside her bed. 'Beaut,' I lied.

Looking ahead through my bow wave, I see the glint of blue tile.

In the end it's instinct that determines which hand will touch, plus a few years' experience! Maggie's flip I know to be neater, with her shorter legs, and more reliable; mine is less dependable, but when it really works, fantastic.

It's that sort I need. Right now. The right hand touches, slides down the wall. Follow it down, legs shoot over. If it's a good one, feet will be close to the wall for a good strong push-off.

I'm over! I've seen a flash of black in the lane next door. My legs thrust backwards, hopefully sending me off towards the finish like a catapult. I'm Archer and Arrow again, taut from fingertip to toetip.

But you've slipped, Alex! Your toes have not gripped the wall. Your push-off makes the best of a bad job, but is feeble compared with what it could have been. An eighty per cent push. Your leg reminds you that a few months ago it had problems of its own. You know without looking that the black torpedo in the *next lane has done one of its neat, reliable turns and thrust itself into the lead.*

Damn you, Maggie. And damn you even more, Alex's feet, for costing you the trip to Rome. Six years' work, sliding sideways off a patch of tile.

All you watching and yelling people, cheer for me no longer.

Alex has blown it. I can just hear the radio announcer . . . 'They've turned, Miss Archer just slightly ahead, a magnificent first lap, under thirty seconds, there could be a record here, no it's Miss Benton who comes out in front, what a magnificent turn, half a yard ahead now as they begin to stroke . . .'

Alex has blown it. She is screaming and crying too, with anger and shame. You fool!

The first stroke, a breath because my lungs are bursting and there's worse to come, and even though Maggie is now on my blind side I can see enough out of the corner of my right eye to know that she has a full yard on me.

I'm sorry, Andy. My gift—resolutions, intentions, determinations—was not enough.

5

It's not every day your city declares open the harbour bridge it has been dreaming about for a hundred years, planning for over ten and building over five. The week after Maggie's dance we talked, read, heard about nothing else in the newspapers, on radio: our new bridge that some thought was more elegant than Sydney's, and others thought looked like a coathanger, and with only four lanes was going to be too small even before it was opened, and shame that they'd had to do away with footpaths so people couldn't walk over and admire the view. Rows of smug old men—mayors and politicians, city council and harbour board members—stared daily out of the newspapers. I noted that one of them was called P. N. R. Allardyce and had exactly the same self-satisfied expression as his nephew.

Andy had been right about Maggie and her dance. She'd hated every minute of it, she told me at training two days later in an unusual burst of confidence.

'I'd have given anything to take my shoes off too, but you know what Mother's like. She made me get these English shoes. Looked nice, but hurt, even in the shop. Two other girls had broken heels . . .' (So I wasn't the only one) '. . . and one broke her bra strap and we couldn't find a safety pin. They were all

73

so embarrassed they went home.' (What?) 'Then Briar, from my class, lost her petticoat completely. The elastic went. Christopher Allardyce, her partner' (oh yes?) 'was so embarrassed he left her in the middle of the floor and she had to step out of it and pick it up and screw it into a little bundle, which wasn't very little, all those gathers and frills and hoops and stiff net and stuff, and walk off all by herself. At least he could have danced her to the side, somewhere near the Ladies, the swine.'

'Poor her,' I said. 'I met Christopher, very proper he was. In fact, a proper drongo.' We were getting dressed, leisurely for once, because Maggie was clearly needing to get it all off her chest to someone.

'He wanted to know who the American girl was, the tall one, with the legs like a chorus girl. Danced like Cyd Charisse, he said. Beat's me—well, he'd had a few, whiskies and that, with the adults. He got very angry when he heard Briar had already gone home with some friends. Don't blame her, do you? Then some guy had an asthma attack and had to be taken home, and someone else's partner arrived drunk and started to abuse the waiters, and then we had to throw out two carloads of gatecrashers. Susan's Dad took charge, threatened to call the police. Trouble is, they were friends of Susan's, you know . . . And my silly mother is saying if that's supposed to be the best band in Auckland she'll eat her hat and she asked them not to play rock 'n' roll and they did, and she's threatening not to pay the caterers because there wasn't enough food.'

Her silly *what?* I looked at her in the mirror as we both slicked down our wet hair, astonished. 'There was plenty of food, Maggie. And I thought the band was great.'

'So did I. Trouble is, Mother thinks she's still in Singapore. She gave lots of parties there, cocktails at the club and that. Always sitting around drinking gin. I wasn't sorry to leave.'

Well! Behind the scenes of what I'd taken to be a typical dance, overdone with formality and starch, had been all sorts of dramas. Was life always in layers, like water, clear on the surface but more murky and dramatic and complicated the deeper you got? I still couldn't work out why they bothered, people like Maggie's mum. Who were they trying to impress?

'Sorry, I didn't mean to . . .' said Maggie.

'Sorry for what?'

'All that about my awful dance. Boring really. But at school, that's all they talk about, dances, gossip . . . With you, here, it's a relief, I don't have to . . .'

'Try so hard?'

She nodded, embarrassed. 'Thanks,' I said. 'I'll take that as a compliment.' But I knew what she was trying to say. Here in the pool, in the water, among our swimming friends who were a pretty mixed bunch, she could be herself, judged on her own terms, not those set by her mother or the private school she went to. Minus all the trappings, we met as equals.

The boys' school Sixth Form dance was a much less stuffy affair, with no over-dressed parents hanging around and only a small disturbance by some gatecrashers, which the teachers on patrol dealt with swiftly. There was a great band, Bill Haley-style rock 'n' roll music, very loud, nearly all night. Andy and I danced ourselves into the ground. I knew lots of girls from my school. Dress went all the way from diamante, strapless and gloves, to circular skirts or even a few jeans, pony-tails, cardigans worn back to front and eyelids full of liner. Gran had made me an emerald green skirt to wear with a slinky black top, a four-inch wide black elastic belt, and I borrowed Mum's black low-heeled shoes, plain as ballet shoes, ideal for twirling.

I enjoyed this dance as much as I'd hated Maggie's. Three days after hearing all those awful things the hurt remained, but only as a dull ache somewhere deep inside. Let them think what they pleased. Dancing with Andy was all I needed, getting lost in the pulse of the music, looking only for his eyes and the strong hand which would propel me into yet another pirouette.

It all started, really, that night, not with anything soppy like whether or not he opened car doors for me (we'd agreed I was perfectly capable of opening my own) or the way he said goodbye at the front door (just another hug), but in the shared exhilaration of the dance. And going home he suggested we do the 'Great Once-Only Walk' across the new bridge the following day.

Half the city was expected, but it seemed as though the *whole* city had turned out, well wrapped up against the cold south-westerly wind. We kept bumping into people we knew, swimming and school friends; even Mr Jack and his equally buxom wife who ran the pool tuckshop and was known to us all as Mrs Jill, both puffing from the long walk up one side and down the other. Not Maggie. She'd hinted at training that morning that in her household 'The Walk' was being regarded as an exercise for hoi polloi; besides, her mother thought it was bad for her swimmer's legs to walk that far. 'Come with Andy and me,' I suggested, but a trip had been arranged to visit relatives on a farm near Hamilton.

We walked right over, about two miles, to the toll plaza and back up to the top, where we stopped to lean over the rail. The water shimmered a long way beneath. It would be so easy just to swing a leg over the rail and fly off, join the seagulls below.

'Would you live, do you think?' I said.

'Might. D-depend on the way you hit. As hard as concrete, they say, from this height. Imagine your thoughts, going down. I can think of pleasanter ways to d-d-snuff it.'

We looked across to the city's gentle green hills. 'Last, loneliest, loveliest, exquisite, apart . . .'

'Who said that?'

'Rudyard Kipling, about Auckland. A poem called "Song of the Cities". He did a grand t-tour of the Empire in 1891. My English teacher's mad on Kipling, trots it out in his best Gielgud. Rest of it's pretty dreary. There's better Kipling.

If you can keep your head when all about you
Are losing theirs and blaming it on you . . .

77

He went on, through the whole thing . . .

If you can fill the unforgiving minute
With sixty seconds worth of distance run,
Yours is the Earth and everything that's in it,
And—which is more—you'll be a Man, my son!

He laughed. 'Sorry about that, Alex. Girls didn't run, let alone swim, in Kipling's d-day. And no one needs to tell you how to fill your unforgiving minute.'

'Sixty seconds worth of distance swum would be more like it.' The amazing view of the harbour, this clever person beside me who could quote Kipling and win prizes for physics and play the trumpet and wanted to go to sea, despite what his father thought, it all went to my head. I felt reckless and exhilarated. I grabbed Andy's hand. 'Let's run down.' We went haring off down towards the city side, dodging among the crowd, which by now had thinned a bit, shouting greetings to friends we saw in the opposite two lanes. Grannies smiled at us, as they did to children. Our pace dropped to a brisk walk. I realized I was still holding his hand. And enjoying it.

The car was miles away. The road got steeper, and though we were both breathless, I was puffing less.

'You'd better come back to training,' I said.

'That's a sore point. No swimming, no skiing at August, no more trumpet. I'm allowed to play rugby this year, that's all.'

'That's crazy. You'd stay fitter if you kept on swimming. What about injuries? You go and dislocate your shoulder or something? Or get your head stamped on, at the bottom of a scrum.'

'You know the old man.'

Bad-tempered, bossy, not quite an All Black in his day, forever talking about Springboks and Lions and the team he didn't quite make in 1928 or whenever, and his latest golf score. I knew him. Determined that Andy was going to scale the ultimate twin pinnacles of New Zealand manhood, as a doctor *and* an All Black, and all outside activities during this scholarship year forbidden to that end.

'I'm surprised he let you out twice this week to go to the dances,' I said.

'He d-didn't. He's away, on business, and Mum, well . . . she's all for a bit of social life. And someone's got to look after you.'

'I beg your pardon. I can look after myself very well.'

'So sure? You worry me.'

'Why?'

'Your swimming's one thing, what about all the rest. Maggie *only* swims. Hasn't anyone ever t-t-said you could beat her hands-down every time if you *only* swam?'

'Mr Jack has hinted as much. Dad . . .'

'Only hinted? He's supposed to be your coach, for heaven's sake.' His hand was gripping mine tightly.

'Mr Jack understands, that's why he's a good coach. He doesn't think the world starts and finishes with swimming . . . neither do I . . .'

'It does for Maggie. And her parents. That's why she keeps winning.'

'He knows me, that I have to . . .'

'Be all things to all people?'

I yanked my hand from his grip. 'It's not that. I just . . . like being *in* things. It's important.'

'Why?'

'Well, I might be asking some questions too, like why are you letting your old man run your life, putting his foot down about this and that . . . everything except rugby which is the most stupid dangerous game ever invented, guaranteed to land you up in hospital sooner or later . . .'

'OK, you tell me.'

'Because he's got great plans for you. "You'll be a Man, My Son!" Except that he doesn't know that you have no intention of trying for medical school and boy, are you in for . . .'

'Don't shift it all on to Dad, Alex. You don't do me justice when you say that. I've got my own plans. I've got to get accepted into the Navy first. I wasn't much of a trumpeter so that doesn't matter. Skiing will wait, so will swimming till next season. And rugby's not so horribly dangerous, senior club's a bit rough, perhaps, but not school . . .'

'I hate it.'

'You're just jealous.'

'I wouldn't waste my time.'

'Anyway, you're side-stepping.'

'I'm not.'

'Why hasn't your old man put his foot down with you, then, or your mum, who can be as solid as a rock when she chooses?'

'Because, because . . .'

'Because they know you wouldn't listen. Or they don't take your ambitions very seriously? They know, *I* know you want to do law. And what about the Olympics next year?'

'They do take me seriously! No one else does much, but they do. Look I'm only Fifth Form. You're doing scholarship. Give me a chance!'

'Breeze through School Cert. Breeze through University Entrance, breeze through life. Yeah, you will, Alex, because you're you, for a while.'

In the silence he took my hand again. We'd reached the car.

'Whether you'll breeze your way into the Games team is another matter. Has it occurred to you that you might not?'

'Of course it has. Where do you think I've been all these years? Second, time and time again.' You're a liar, Alex Archer. You do expect to beat Maggie, when the chips are down next February. You keep telling yourself that when you *really* start trying . . .

'But up till now there has not been too much at stake, has there?' he persisted.

'Only a medal or a title or a record or two.'

'Not a black blazer, a trip to Rome. How badly do you want it? I sometimes wonder. You know, I do worry about you, Alex Archer,' he said gently. Leaning forward he pinned me up against the side of the car and kissed me. On the mouth.

Back to school for the winter term, traffic jamming up daily on the new bridge, six am training now part of my daily routine—and strife not two days into the first week.

On the Hockey notice-board was the list of people selected for the First Eleven. My name was not there.

Some mistake, surely? In the place I'd mentally reserved for myself, right half, was B. Selwyn: Sixth Former. Last year in the Second team, stolid enough but *no* dash, no inspiration, just a reliable stick that stopped balls, and fed them back to the forwards. I'd shot a few goals from right half last season, which I doubted she'd done.

Underneath I noticed the Second Eleven, with A. Archer as right half.

'Barbara Selwyn? Well, what d'ya know!' I heard Julia's voice saying, dimly.

'None other,' I said.

'But you were a dead cert.'

'Apparently not.' I was now seeing through hot eyes that two or three from my last year's Junior team had made it straight into the First. I'd seen enough. 'I've got a rehearsal, see you.'

Julia came after me. 'Alex, that's not fair. Even I can see Barbara's not exactly nifty on her pins.'

'Apparently she's better,' I said walking fast through the lunch-time groups, and unintentionally straight past Miss Edwards who had done this to me. Julia, sensing that I wanted to be left alone, didn't try to keep up. I nearly turned on the spur of the moment to ask Miss Edwards why she'd chosen Barbara ahead of me, but pride said, don't ask for more hurt, Alex. I could give up hockey altogether, but it might look as though I'd given up in a huff, and I didn't want that to be said. And I enjoyed it too much to give up. It only meant two practices a week and a game on Saturday mornings.

At the first practice game before school the next day, I lined up with the Second team, chirpy as they come. Made nice noises to Barbara, who obviously could hardly believe her luck, and played like a demon. There was no chance of my team beating the First, but I put our only goal in the net. Put that in your pipe, Miss Edwards.

'Played well, Alex,' she said, as we stumbled muddily from the field, red-faced and panting, me less than most. 'Could you stay behind a moment?'

It turned into a monologue. 'You might be a little disappointed, Alex. I imagine you'd hoped to make the First team this winter. But you do have two more seasons at school, assuming you're staying into Upper Sixth, and Barbara is in her last year. Admittedly, she's not as fast or as fit as you, but she's very reliable and works hard and it means a lot to her. Also we felt that with all your activities both in and out of school, you have enough pressure as it is, and in the Second Eleven you can enjoy your hockey without the strain . . .'

I heard her out, mumbled a few understanding noises, which made her feel better, and probably kidded her that I was not hurting all the way down to the toes of my muddy boots. Yes, Miss Edwards, I'm very used to being second best, Miss Edwards, but in swimming I'm second best to a top-flight lady. I'm also regarded by some as a second best specimen of

83

femininity around the place—except that Andy not only kissed me so many times I lost count on that day of the bridge walk, but also, later in the car, very gently traced the outline of my breast with his fingers, deliciously reassuring me of my femininity . . .

Actually, what I'm really getting tired of is people who think they know what is best for me. Andy's well-meaning, no doubt, but he's three years older. Does life have to get so serious in the Fifth Form? And there's Mr Jack, asking bluntly when I turned up to training one morning with a massive bruise on my shin, had I considered giving up hockey this winter, given the risk of injuries, and did I want to give myself a fair crack at Rome? A Greek chorus from Dad in the car on the way home. Even Mum, more subtle again, and Gran sighing into her cup of tea everytime I helped her with her sewing, which admittedly was not very often, 'You're so busy, Alex, so busy. I don't know how you keep going, I just don't.'

Yet they supported me, to the hilt, all of them, and Rome was miles away yet. Dad enjoyed coming to training with me before dawn; he swam too, while I trained, and said the exercise was good for him. We came home to cereal and Mum's steaming cooked breakfast, eggs, bacon, sausages, fried bread. Before school to hockey practices, lunch-times to rehearsals, after school to piano or ballet. Early meals so that I would have the evenings free for homework and piano practice. I was let off drying dishes, which I knew irked all the kids, especially Jamie, who's about as loud-mouthed a twelve-year-old boy as you'll find anywhere, but they dried them just the same.

Then one Saturday morning early in June I collected a really vicious ball at close range from a stick wielded by a twelve-ton Tessie. The whole team from some country school up north was big, like me, but this girl playing left back outdid all of us, and when she took a swipe at the ball, watch out. It rose above the mud and landed just behind the pad on the side of my right leg, and when I came back to earth and tried to pick myself up and found I couldn't walk things really started to come unstuck.

The doctor at casualty didn't look much older than Andy, but he had black smudges under his eyes, and his hands, as he ran them over my leg, seemed to be shaking slightly, which Mum told me later came from working over ninety hours a week as a house surgeon and being on call practically all the time and paid an absolute pittance.

'Comminuted fracture of the fibula,' he intoned, peering up at the X-ray. The pompous manner and glasses didn't go with the haircut, which was almost a teddy boy's duck's tail. 'Fortunately the bone is in good alignment. Plaster for six to eight weeks will be necessary.' He might have been reading today's sharemarket prices.

'It can't be. What's comminuted?'

'It is. Comminuted means several cracks. See for yourself.' He pointed to the paler lines on the X-ray. I looked down at my swollen leg, plum-coloured, horribly aching and still muddy, then up at Dad.

'It *can't* be, please.' I felt Dad's hand on my shoulder.

'Young lady, when I tell you your fibula's sustained a comminuted fracture and that plaster from foot to above the knee is necessary, that's exactly what I mean.' He was now looking at me squarely for the first time. The panic in my eyes must have stirred up something from the depths of his weariness. 'I played hockey myself once, with similar results. I'm sorry.'

He started writing on his bits of paper, then looked up. 'Alexandra Archer? Are you the girl who swims?'

I nodded, head down so that he couldn't see my eyes, as the implications began to sink in. No hockey, no ballet, no training even. Maybe out of the production at the end of term. Staggering around on crutches. All for a lousy Second Eleven match against a brutal lot of overgrown country bumpkins. I felt sick.

'Swimming's the best thing to get your leg back into shape when all this is over,' he said more gently. 'Are you training at the moment?'

'I was until today.'

'Get yourself a good physiotherapist. Couple of months, you'll be back in the water. Now, the nurse will wheel you into plaster room.'

'Couple of months!' I cried to Dad later as he helped me, weighted down with a plaster from knee to toe, out to the car. 'Couple of *months*!'

Andy came around later in the afternoon. I was reclining in state on my bed, flowers arranged by Mum, Dad's transistor radio to hand, fresh grapefruit juice, a bell in case I needed anything, and kids and/or Gran coming when I rang. Very sorry for myself.

'Your dad rang me. Bad luck,' he said. He was standing back from the bed because various brats were sniggering in the hall outside.

I shrugged, feeling somewhat foolish. Recently, it was me giving him advice about risks of injury. He would not have forgotten.

'Or a slight relief?'

'What's that supposed to mean?'

'Accidents can make d-d-decisions easier for you.'

'Shit, Andy, so you think I decided to have an accident? You think I *chose* to stand in the path of that over-sized bullet and bugger up my ballet, the school show, not to mention my training and the little matter of Rome next year?'

'Not exactly . . .'

'If that's all you can say I'd rather you didn't come.'

'OK, I'm sorry, tactless, heartless, cruel, all that. I'm truly sorry, Alex. Is it sore?'

'Yeah. And *boring*.' I'd not cried, really cried, to anyone yet, to Dad or Mum or Gran fussing around, and certainly not in front of the kids, and I'd not meant to cry in front of Andy. But tears came from nowhere and I just couldn't help it.

He said nothing for about five minutes, but just held my hand at first. Then when the waterworks went on and on, he got up and shut the door so that no prying eyes would see him give me a long strong cuddle, smoothing back my hair, planting kiss after kiss on my wet brow.

He was right, of course: part of me was rejoicing.

Two whole months' relief from climbing out of bed in total blackness at five thirty, from eyes being gouged by chlorine; permanent respite from the Second Eleven hockey team. The other part of me knew only too well that come the next nationals Maggie would have two months' more training on the clock, and no matter how hard I trained I might never catch up.

'If you're ahead after the turn, don't let up. If you're not, my only advice is put your head down and gofurrit.'

I am now goingfurrit, Mr Jack, truly I am. Breathing every second stroke, because I've used up nearly all my puff on the first lap and the going's getting rough.

This part of the race I loathe. The tops of your arms are aching, and every breath is your last gasp and you've yet to go into the overdrive where you forget you're dying and the only thing that's left in the world is getting to that solid wall at the end.

There's always the stupid hope that Maggie will somehow slow down, take a mouthful, hit a lane-rope, get a stomach cramp—anything. But she never does. She swims like a true pro. As Andy says, 'That's why she keeps winning, because swimming is her life.'

Hasn't it been my life? So much so that I've been obsessed by it, even to the point of not noticing that Gran was fading away to a shadow, and Julia had *just a wee problem with that Australian uncle of hers.*

I'm not going to make it. It's all been too much, really. I'm retiring as of now. Good luck for Rome, Maggie. I'll find someone who's got a television and watch you on that.

Don't give in, Alex. Never give in. Forty yards to go yet.

Andy, have pity.

I can't keep this up.

6

I had long known that Dad and Mr Jack had little chats about me and my training on the phone or while I was ploughing up and down the pool, but the Monday after my plaster went on, Mr Jack came around in the evening and there was a big chat in the front room.

Eventually I was called in, by this time quite wound up. They both looked very solemn as I swung my crutches through the doorway and eased myself on to a chair. Mr Jack was shaking his head slightly as though he couldn't quite believe what he was seeing.

'Evening, Mr Jack.'

I got a rueful smile. 'Well, Alex, where do we go from here?'

'I'm not going anywhere, am I? Well, I went to school today and very boring it was too, answering the same question over and over again. I can't train for six weeks and my ballet teacher has had a go at Mum because I can't be in her recital in October, and Miss Edwards at school is feeling all guilty and . . .'

'Alex . . .'

'. . . and my piano teacher is angry because it was my right leg and not my left and if it had only been my left I could have worked the pedal and taken my exam and . . .'

'Alex!'

'. . . I can't do gym or calisthenics or go to any dances or places.' I could hear myself burbling on like the babbling brook. 'All I can do is boring homework and play the piano without the pedal and twiddle my toes. Oh no, that's not all, I can't be the Scarecrow in *The Wizard of Oz,* but I can be the Tinman because he's stiff-legged anyway and Miss Macrae, who's producing the show, said today that what you lose on the swings you gain on the roundabouts . . .'

I petered out. Smiles, the patronizing adult sort, were being exchanged.

'Alexandra Archer, would you do me a favour?' said Mr Jack quietly.

'Anytime.'

'Pull your head in. Stop talking and listen.'

'Sure.' I was on uncertain ground here.

'It's June, June the eighth to be precise, 1959. Right?'

I nodded, despite myself, I was interested in what was coming.

'The nationals are next February, right? The nominations for Rome will be sometime after that? Now, those dates aren't going to change. No one and nothing's going to wait for your leg to get better or you to . . .'

'I never thought they would.'

'No, but do you realize you've only seven months to prepare for those nationals. *Seven* months, from now.'

Put like that, I hadn't, but I also wasn't going to let on.

'In that time you've got to work your leg back into shape, put in some solid training and sit School Certificate. Your father has made it quite clear, between August and October, exams will come first. After that you've got about three and a half months.'

'What we are saying, Alex,' said Dad, 'is this. If you want to get to Rome, you must plan now. Because of this little set-back, ballet and hockey are out. They should stay out, at least this year.'

I was silent. All this seriousness was getting to me. And give up ballet? Didn't they know how much I loved dancing?

Mr Jack said, 'Alex, do you want that trip to Rome?'

I nodded.

'How badly?' he persisted.

'Badly. But . . .'

'Before you go any further, I'd better say that all this was probably a blessing in disguise.'

'Hardly.'

'Your father has asked me for my considered opinion of your chances next February. Well, here it is, straight. Three silvers, but not close enough to Maggie to be considered for Rome.'

'You'd coach me, thinking that?'

'Sure. I'd do my professional best for you. But there's only so much I can do or say. It's basically up to you.'

The genial smile and twinkling eyes had gone. He was in dead earnest.

'So, I think it's time for you to tell me, no, both your father and me, just how much you are prepared to give up.'

After a pause I said, 'I don't actually have much choice, do I?' I sounded surly, but I was not enjoying being put on the spot.

'In the long term, you have plenty. In the short—yes, you still have some,' said Mr Jack. 'You can't train in the water, but you can train out of it. We can work on a programme of weights, use these weeks to strengthen arms and upper body. We'll need good physio advice when the plaster comes off. The hockey team will manage without you, your ballet teacher's recital likewise. And you can get more shuteye than usual.'

My eyes met Dad's briefly. Mr Jack clearly knew quite a bit about my home life, more than I imagined. My late nights, usually catching up on homework or music theory, were a source of some friction between me and Mum. She was a night owl herself, and she'd see the light on under my door and come prowling in asking how much more I had to do. I always halved the estimated time and hoped she wouldn't notice, but I suspect she did.

'You say . . . I wouldn't have beaten Maggie at the nationals . . . ?' I said.

'Not unless you cut down, no. You might have surprised me,' he added with a slight smile, 'as you've surprised me before.'

'*If* I do as you've planned it all out . . . with Dad . . . what are my chances?'

'Good.'

'Just . . . good? That's all?'

'What more can I say? I can't say yes, Alex, you'll beat her hands down, your chances are great, because you know as well as I do that Maggie's a tough little cookie and she's got the advantage of a mother who's prepared to work hard and fight hard and spend money to see her daughter on the victory dais. Maggie is single-minded and a worker, and she doesn't bend under pressure. Your advantage is your greater natural talent, your height, your long limbs and . . . I'm bound to say, your talents in directions other than swimming. A buoyant personality, which can count when the chips are down. Many outstanding athletes are just that, rather special people. They often go on to success in other fields. You will, in due course.'

Such eloquence rather bowled me over. I sat quietly, trying to take all this in.

'So it's not going to be easy, Alex. And I can't guarantee success. You might do all we ask of you, and still see Maggie as the only nomination for Rome.'

'I'm going to be two months' training behind her, for a start . . .'

'Only in a sense. OK, this is a set-back, but all the years you've put in already, they're not wasted, Alex. Your hockey training, the suppleness and control from ballet, rhythm from your music, all helps . . .'

'Oh good,' I said somewhat bitterly; my leg was aching and it sounded like I had a pretty uphill battle ahead of me.

Mr Jack stood up. 'Think about it. You don't have to make any decisions right now, Alex, except one. Do you want to start on weights next week?'

'Yes.' I didn't hesitate. All this sitting around talking was driving me bananas.

'Good. I'll get some equipment, and a programme nutted out. Thanks Jim, see myself out. Don't get up, Alex. T.T.F.N.'

'Ta-ta for now,' I called. Dad saw him off, with more chat out at the car, while I sat on, thinking, my Tinman's leg stuck out to one side. I had much to think about.

I was not, according to Mum as nurse, a good patient. I bored the whole family rigid complaining about having to be helped into a bath and being driven to school and having to ask someone to carry my schoolbag. In winter, between classrooms, between home and school, there was the problem of keeping plaster dry and toes warm. People horsed around with my crutches, and drew silly pictures on my cast. I had to sleep with my leg on a pillow. Later I had to poke down inside the cast with a knitting needle to get at itches.

Sympathy became boring too. I hated being so conspicuous in assemblies and getting on buses, and I have to admit that more than a few people got a thick ear when they tried to help. Wobbly at first, I soon learnt to speed along the school corridors faster than people could walk.

I wasn't seeing much of Andy, who was head down into books and rugby scrums. At home I sat for long periods in my room, listening to the Goon Show and working away with the weights Mr Jack had brought around. I could do lots of floor exercises like bending from the waist, frontwards, sideways, back, or lifting my torso off the floor and holding; or even lifting my legs and holding—murder on stomach muscles with the extra weight of the cast.

Not rushing out to training at five thirty, I had time to listen to my radio when I woke. On the early news, it was rugby and the All Blacks all the time, a real blow-up because they'd announced that the team going to South Africa next year would be without any Maori players, to keep the South Africans happy. There'd been a petition and a march on Parliament by six hundred students in Wellington and it seemed there wasn't any middle ground. Either you thought the arrangement was OK, or you thought the team shouldn't be going at all under those terms.

Andy and I, to his father's disgust, shared the opinion that the team shouldn't be going.

'And protestors, students, dangerous riff-raff should all be locked up,' his father stated during a steamy discussion in the Richmond kitchen. The three of us were doing the dishes after a Sunday roast with all the trimmings. With Andy being an only child, meals at his place were quiet adult affairs, with English china and napkins in polished silver rings and butter knives, unlike the noisy battlefield that I was used to at home.

'Because they're standing up and being counted? Come on, Dad,' said Andy.

'Politics shouldn't be brought into sport,' droned Mr Richmond for about the eighth time, rubbing the Spode dinner plate ever more vigorously. If you haven't been to South Africa . . .'

'. . . you've no right to pass judgement,' joined in Andy.

'Just so.'

'Dad, why should we have to conform to their rules?'

'Because we are their visitors, their guests. Because it is the best arrangement for all concerned, including our Maoris themselves.'

'Imagine how you'd feel if you were one of the Maoris left out, after all that training,' I said.

'You'd be old enough to understand the complexity . . .'

'I don't think it's complex at all. I think it's very simple,' I said.

'Really.'

'It's a New Zealand team, isn't it? We send our best team, just like we do to the Olympics. If the South Africans don't like who we select, that's their . . .'

'A simplistic line of reasoning. Fallacious. Quite unrealistic.' He was going to blind me with words.

'If I thought my hard training all went for nothing because a lot of politicians . . .'

He laughed. 'Oh, I know you're a good swimmer, sweetie, but what would you know of training?'

'Pardon?'

'You young things, kids, slips of girls, you don't know what training is. A few lengths of a pool, I daresay. A spot of sunbathing in your bikinis.'

'Dad . . .'

I waved him down. There was a dangerous silence. 'Tell me about training, Mr Richmond.'

'We'd come in, every muscle aching, covered with mud, exhausted . . .'

'. . . but happy,' I put in politely.

'Exactly. Seven o'clock in the morning and the frost not even off the grounds. Passing practice, line-outs, until you're bent double. Practice after dark, mud and rain. A sense of trust in your teammates . . .'

'Real man's work,' I said.

He looked at me suspiciously. My face was as blank as I could make it. Inside I was shouting '*balls*!'

'Well, time I went, Andy,' I said, hanging up my damp tea-towel and slotting crutches under armpits. I hoped I could contain my anger until I got outside, before I said something really rude, or threw a plate at him. 'Goodbye, Mr Richmond. Excuse me, but I must go and', I couldn't resist, 'do some real girl's work.'

He looked around from re-lighting his pipe.

'Lifting weights, about two hundred pounds each. Didn't you know they're introducing women's weight-lifting at the Olympics next year?'

I had the satisfaction of seeing the lighted match pause and his mouth drop, just a little. For a moment I think he might have believed me.

'Alex, wait,' said Andy as I swung off down the path on my crutches, somewhat in danger of over-reaching myself and ending in a heap on the road. He was still wiping his hands on the frilly yellow apron. 'Pay no attention . . .'

'I don't.'

'He doesn't know what he's talking about.'

'I'll say. That rot about *real* training . . .'

'Look, you know he knows nothing about it. He

took no interest in my swimming, never came to the pool once, not one carnival. He's never seen a training session in his life.'

'I bet he comes to *all* your rugby games.'

'Yes, and after years of shouting at me from the sideline even he's beginning to realize I'm not going to be another d-d-Don Clarke.'

Interesting. A male version of Mrs Benton.

'I can open my own car door, thank you.'

Somehow I managed door, crutches, getting inside, hauling crutches in after me. Andy watched initially, then shrugged and went around to get in the driver's seat. By the time he had started up the car I was laughing.

'Did you *see* the expression on his face as we left. I shouldn't tease him, but . . . Oh hell, I forgot to thank your mother for lunch.'

'She won't mind. I'll tell her. I think she's quite glad that somebody argues with the old man other than me. She gave up years ago.'

We laughed all the way home. No, that's not strictly true, we took a slight detour and parked behind a tree in the park. Thirty minutes of kissing and petting (not heavy, the lighter version), and I went home in the best humour I'd been in for days.

Although we talked about the All Black row in the cloakrooms at school, with most of us thinking along much the same lines, in class it hardly rated a mention. An All Black team was going to South Africa minus a few Maoris, so what? Girls' schools hardly need concern themselves with male sports, even the one that everyone agreed was the country's national religion, and Maori culture was an annual trip to see the canoe in the museum. Miss Gillies was more concerned with getting through the exam syllabus. In English, where current events were sometimes discussed, Miss Hunt was currently putting us all to sleep with her very correct readings of *The Mill on the Floss* and Gray's 'Elegy in a Country Churchyard'.

Most of us were connected in some way with *The Wizard of Oz*, since the school prided itself on its productions. Through July we rehearsed three lunchtimes a week and one afternoon after school. My mishap had thrown Miss Macrae only temporarily off balance. 'My dear Alex, my Scarecrow,' she had boomed when I hobbled into rehearsal the week after the break. 'You auditioned so brilliantly. Where will I find another Scarecrow?'

Miss Macrae was in her Laurence Olivier as Hamlet pose, hand to brow, musing. She wore plain suits, a Joan of Arc hairstyle, and her voice (in the best British tradition, trained at the Royal Academy of Dramatic Art) could be heard all over the school.

'Tinman, that's it,' she declaimed. 'You can be the Tinman. We can paint your plaster cast silver.'

'I'll be out of it long before that.'

'How long?' Not only did she look like Joan of Arc might have done if she'd reached fifty, she had once played Joan on the London stage. That was about all we knew. How she'd ended up teaching Dramatic Art at a girls' school in Auckland, New Zealand, none of us ever found out. 'But you'll not be dancing, I fear. Not Scarecrow dancing.'

'Doubt it.'

'Janice can be Scarecrow. She'll make quite a good fist of it, I daresay. If your leg's up to it, we'll put in an extra dance for you.'

I was not thrilled. I thought the Tinman a creep, unlike the Scarecrow, who was a character of some spunk. And every time I'd seen the film, which was now four, it had disturbed me that the Tinman actor had nearly died because of all the toxic silver stuff they had used on his skin. But as with the Second Eleven hockey I felt certain obligations, stupidly, and I was enjoying the whole production far too much to pull out now.

So Tinman I was. I somehow failed to tell them at home until we were into the round of full run-throughs coming up to dress rehearsals in August. Eyebrows went up into heads when I started mentioning weekend rehearsals, and Jamie made rude comments about me supposedly cutting down on my activities, including pulling out of the school show. I would have been wiser not to take on Tinman. But I was in too deep.

The grand ceremony of taking off the plaster, scheduled for the second week of July, was an anti-climax. At the hospital there was much fuss with X-rays and cautionary pep talks from yet another young doctor suffering from exhaustion. In the plaster room an orderly with arms like a truck driver and Elvis kiss curls expertly wielded a gigantic pair of hedge clippers. On the slab all lay revealed. A pathetic shrivelled leg, hairy, pale, scaly and noticeably smaller than the other. Also two knitting needles I'd lost in my frantic poking for an itch. 'Ugh' I thought, then 'Aaaaaah' as I had a good scratch. If I thought I could put on a shoe and walk out, I had a shock coming. A nurse rolled bandage around my leg from knee down. Then it was crutches again, peg-legging it down the hospital steps.

I was so impatient to get training again, that if I'd known then that it would be another three weeks of bandage, crutches, and sessions with the physio, I'd probably have stepped under a bus there and then.

I knew now it was the water I had missed more than anything. I needed that swirl of water around my body, the actual touch of cool water on skin, the feeling of flying, of lightness, and of power. Even on my least inspired days of training, I always had a little frolic, dolphin-diving in the shallow end, or a long moment of lying on my back, weightless. They say our bodies are two-thirds water, but water seemed to have got into my soul, too. When I couldn't swim, I felt starved.

At the end of the second week, I became so desperate I made Andy put down his books for an hour and drive me to the pool for a swim. On a quiet Sunday afternoon I hoped no one else we knew would be there. We unwound the bandage in the car and I tried to walk into the pool as normally as possible.

Cleopatra in her asses' milk had nothing on me. With Andy hovering around to make sure I didn't slip on the wet concrete, I got to the side of the pool and dangled my legs into the water. Beside me Andy sat, too. If he'd known what I was thinking he would have run a mile, but this was the first swim we'd had together since . . . since we'd moved on to the kissing plane. All that distance, those years we'd trained together, but today I was bowled over by his beauty when he stood on the block, dived cleanly in, did a lap and came back to slither the last few yards under water and emerge like a water-god at my feet. This beautiful boy, not quite a man, wants to kiss me, share himself with me, loves me? I could hardly believe my luck. 'Come on,' he said, smiling. That was a swim I shall always remember. Slipping into the shallow end, feeling the cool water slither up my back, over my shoulders, through my hair, I wondered how I could have gone for so long. It felt like a million years. I did a few laps without kicking, taking care to push off with one leg only. Andy swam alongside me. There was only an occasional twinge and we made a reasonable job of putting the bandage back on. I made sure my hair was very dry before I got home.

When Andy suggested a trip to Helensville for a hot swim the following weekend, I got grudging permission from Mum to go, and all sorts of conditions. The chance of another fun swim with Andy was too good to miss. It was to prove another bad decision.

*If you really mean business, you have to keep it up,
Alex, and more.*

*Am I gaining on her, Andy? Pinned her back a
hand's breadth, a finger, a fingernail even?*

*This is for real, maybe the first race in my life at
total one hundred per cent effort, where desperation
and rage have added their fuel to ambition, and
afterwards I will be able to look Mr Jack and Dad
and Mum and Gran and the kids and Miss Gillies and
Maggie and even Mrs Benton in the face and say I
could not have tried harder.*

*Breathing is uphill and every arm stroke a circle of
pain. My legs, shaved so carefully in the shower
tonight, are tingling, almost as though being massaged by the water. It's a feeling I've not had often;
a signal that my body is about to go into another
gear.*

*I think I'm gaining. I can no longer see much. I
dare not upset my rhythm and take a breath to the
right. I never learnt to breathe right-handed. It always felt as awkward as breathing to the left was*

natural. The water is choppy and I can't tell whether the arms and legs flailing away next door are ahead or even with me. But I think I'm gaining.

Andy, tell me, I need to know. Am I? Am I?

7

It wasn't the first time I'd been to the hot springs at Helensville. Every winter, once or twice, we went as a family for a Sunday treat, leaving Gran behind for what she called a nice day's peace and quiet to herself. We'd come home water-logged, cooked like lobsters, the car windows steaming up and Deb and Robbie asleep on the slow journey home in the dark. But this was the first time I'd been allowed to go with friends.

They turned up early Saturday afternoon at the front door—Andy, his friend called Keith Jameson and a tiny smart miss called Vicki, who smoked a cigarette while the rest of us went through the hellos and goodbyes with Dad. Andy had warned me Keith was a gruff, prickly sort of guy, but good value, really, the best maths scholar the school had seen for years, set to be top of the class, and then do engineering next year. He was also rather strange-looking, short with heavy gnomish eyebrows that almost met in the middle.

Andy and I slotted ourselves into the back seat of the pale blue Morris Minor car. Our long thighs lay the only way they could, crossways and close. We hadn't even got to the end of the road before his arm was around me.

We left pleasure behind at the gate though, as Keith was not the relaxed driver that Andy was. Through several orange lights, one which was undoubtedly red, around corners on squealing wheels, nipping out to overtake and back as oncoming cars sped towards us, we were soon hurtling along the country highways. Keith drove that Morris like the Triumph TR3 he said he was saving for.

'You OK? You're very quiet,' murmured Andy. If he was puzzled, so was I. Was this sort of driving normal?

About forty minutes later, although it seemed like forty hours, we pulled up with a scrunch outside the pool complex. As we got out, dust was still rising from where the brakes had grabbed the gravelly road. I felt more than slightly ill. Vicki's cigarettes, and those she had lit for Keith and passed to him without a word, hadn't helped.

For once, the swim failed to work its soothing magic. The thought of the drive home terrified me, even as I felt the relaxing effect of the hot water on my wasted leg, even as Andy pulled me down into the blue for a lengthy underwater kiss until we both had to surface for some fresh air.

In the dressing-room Vicki and I small-talked about her boarding school. She spent quite a bit of time on her face and hair, which she'd not allowed to get wet. When we finally came out, Andy and Keith were sitting at a table with a pile of hamburgers and chips already going cold. 'Women!' sighed Keith. 'Take all day.' Vicki ignored him, and lit another cigarette. I decided to ignore him, too; swimmers, male or female, can change their clothes faster than anyone in this world. They get a lot of practice at it. I ate, listening to talk of their school, the All Black thing, cars, more All Black thing (Keith thought the team should go), more cars, more rugby. It seemed all Keith and Andy had in common was playing in the school First Fifteen.

'I'm not too struck on his driving,' I muttered to Andy as we walked in pairs to the car park. 'Couldn't you drive home?'

After a pause, Andy said, 'He's all right.' Afterwards I learnt that to have made such a suggestion, man to man, would have been a deadly insult.

The sky had clouded over since we were in the pool, and it was trying to rain. We sped past the town's small cluster of houses, shops, garage, dairies, a church; little sign of life except for the pub where, with only fifteen minutes to go before closing time, the six o'clock swill was in full swing. The car park was full and the place inside clearly jammed to the doors with men, getting down as much beer as possible.

'Man, great idea,' said Keith, throwing the wheels into yet another small skid. The car had barely stopped before he was out and gone. 'Come on, Andy, one for the road.'

'Where does that leave us mere females?' I said.

'Sitting waiting for half an hour,' muttered Vicki.

'Won't be long, just get a couple of bottles,' said Andy, hesitating before he walked off towards the sounds of male laughter.

It was a good ten minutes before Andy emerged,

followed a minute or so later by Keith, laughing, swinging a brown paper bag which contained two more bottles. Keith expertly prised off the tops, and handed a bottle over to Andy. Vicki and I were expected to be happy with occasional swigs.

'No thanks,' I said to Andy's offer. He looked a bit sheepish, as well he might. The time had come. 'Keith, could you drive a bit slower, please. I felt sick before.'

He was about to turn the ignition key. 'What?'

Once had taken enough girding of loins, to repeat it took more. 'Could you slow down a bit?'

'Did I hear right?'

'Alex gets carsick,' said Andy hastily.

'Sorry to hear that.' We left the pub behind. 'Just make sure you do it out the window. Mum's car.' Although I was right behind him, I could see his elbow raised for another swig at the bottle. I wished he'd put both hands on the wheel.

I was trying to think what to do or say next when we came around a corner. A farmer and his dog were moving a few cows before nightfall. Vicki saw them momentarily before Keith did, her yell coming just before the howl of the brakes, the skid narrowly missing the dog, and the fearful stop about six inches from a cow's nose. I don't remember the words, only the flow of abuse between the farmer and Keith, who seemed to think that roads were built solely for cars and not cows. Vicki added some surprisingly ripe expressions of her own, about Keith. It would have been funny if I hadn't been so frightened.

'Get your bloody cows off the road,' shouted Keith.

The cows had withdrawn to one side and the car was already accelerating. 'Stupid bastard.'

'Take it easy, Keith,' said Andy.

'Bloody farmers. Think they own the place.'

Over eighty-five miles per hour and I'd reached the end. If I don't get out now, I thought, I'm not going to get home at all.

'Keith, please stop.'

'Why, baby?'

'I'm not your baby and will you please stop.'

'Be sick out the window.'

'No. If you don't stop, I'm going to be sick right over the top of you.'

There was a silence, but no reduction in speed, if anything his foot went down a touch. He flicked the car lights on. Andy's arm was tight around my shoulders.

'Keith . . .'

'Shut up, Vicki.'

'I mean it,' I said. 'Your car will stink for a week. Not to mention you.'

I could almost hear him thinking. He was caught now, between me and Vicki and his mother. His mother's anger won, with her added potential for doing inconvenient things like banning the car. If she knew how he drove, she wouldn't be letting him have the car at all.

'Keith, you'd better stop,' said Vicki. I could feel Andy's tension, and embarrassment too. I was probably breaking all sorts of unwritten male rules.

Of course Keith couldn't just stop like normal people. He threw both his feet at the floor. It wasn't quite a skid, but uncomfortable enough to make his point, with Vicki thrown against the dashboard and Andy and I against the front seats.

Silence, except for a distant dog barking and the car idling. Vicki looked around at me, pulling at her cigarette, scared stiff. Keith was taking another swig of beer. In the rear vision mirror, our eyes met.

'I'm getting out.'

'Suit yourself.'

'I will. I can think of better ways . . .'

He laughed. 'Aren't you going to be sick first?'

'I might, I might not. When I've got my bag out of the back, you can go.'

I looked back inside at Andy. I could hear his mind ticking over, too. Go with her, bad leg and all? or lose face with his mates? No doubt Keith would tell all of them over a beer how Andy had gone after some feeble jittery *girl*. You've got about three seconds, Andy old chum—but I was also pleading for support. After two and a half seconds, I got it.

'Hang on,' he said levering himself with some difficulty towards the open door.

'You're not going too?' incredulously, from Keith.

'Yeah.'

'Don't be such a prick. Let her walk.' I wasn't meant to hear the next bit, but I've got these great ears. 'Silly cow.'

'I can't.'

'Why not?'

'For Pete's sake, Keith, she's only just out of plaster. God knows how we're going to get home.'

Keith shrugged and took another swig. 'Your problem.'

'I don't know what's got in to you.'

From the look I saw Vicki give him, I guessed there was some sort of long-running row going on, which would explain much. Their problem. I was past caring, shaking all over and already wet from the light drizzle. I put my parka on, slung the two bags over my shoulder, turned my back on the car and started walking.

'See you Vicki,' I said. 'Hope you get home all right. I hae me doots.' She peered through the windscreen: two huge eyes giving her the look of a startled doll. The car revved off into the dusk; within seconds the red tail lights had disappeared around the next corner.

The noise seemed to take a long time to fade, leaving a damp stillness that suddenly made me feel very lonely, miles from anywhere. I still didn't know how angry Andy was with me, nor did I particularly care. He'd gone with Keith into the pub, hadn't he?

The dog had stopped barking. I continued walking, but slowed as rage and tension seeped out of me. Andy caught me up, firmly relieving me of both the bags and taking my hand. My leg, only two days out of the last bandage, tired quickly. Even walking on the grassy verge I couldn't disguise the sound of a slight limp.

His voice was more resigned than angry. 'Alex, you do make things . . .'

'Difficult?' My voice went up and up. 'Embarrassing? Tiresome? Silly cow? Is that what you think, too? Did you really want to stay in that car and get killed?' I yelled.

'It wasn't as bad as that . . .'

'Oh yes it was. He's an absolute maniac. He'll kill himself one day, you see. And probably a few others as well.'

We walked along in silence. It was already too dark to see anything more than shapes. A warm tide of relief and gratitude went through me when Andy put his arm around my waist and tried to take some of the weight off my leg.

'Thanks, mate.' My face was wet with both rain and tears. A few more steps and I stopped, because I needed the comfort of his strong arms, to reassure myself with a very hard kiss that I was still alive. 'Thanks. For . . .'

'Alexandra.' Like something out of an old silent movie, he put his finger across my lips. 'My Alex.' He started to laugh. 'Alexandra the Great.'

'That was Alexander.'

Some talk of Alexandra, and some of Hercules,
Of Hector and Lysander and such great names
as these.

'Idiot.' Another (wonderful/amazing/unbelievable/incredible) kiss, our bodies pressed hard together all the way down. 'I didn't want to die. Not like that. Nor you.' So why was I still feeling so fearful, for me, for him?

'No.'

'Hold me, Andy. Make me stop shaking.'

It doesn't seem very sensible, remembering in the cold light of day, but we lay down in the wet grass on the side of the road and had a good long and very damp kiss, the drizzle falling on our parkas, our faces, my bare outstretched legs, until the stillness was broken by a car in the distance. We let the first one go. And the second.

When I got out of Keith's car, I knew there were two choices: either walk to a farmhouse or hitch a ride from a passing car into somewhere where we could ring Dad. Weighing up concern for my silly leg against the feeling I never wanted to get in a stranger's car again, the leg won. Andy declined the first three offers of help, men driving home from the pub. The fourth was a woman with a boy about Jamie's age. All we needed was to be dropped off at the next phone box, said Andy, and my father would come and pick us up.

The phone box was near a fish and chip shop in the next small block of shops. Unfortunately we didn't know that there was another fish and chip shop with a very similar name in the next suburb and mistakenly we told Dad only that Keith's car had broken down.

All my memories of that night are now a jumble. Andy and I sat in the warmth of the shop, playing the odd record on the juke box as we got more and more worried about Dad. When he finally turned up we knew at once that there'd been trouble: an accident about four miles back towards the city. The ambulance had already gone when he came across tow trucks, traffic officers, red lights flashing, the wreck of a pale blue Morris Minor, and some sort of farmer's jeep it had collided with. It had taken him a while to find out they'd taken only three off to hospital, two teenagers thrown from the Morris, beer bottles inside, asking for trouble, and the driver of the jeep. The traffic officer couldn't or wouldn't say how badly hurt or what their names were. He'd got confused, poor Dad, in his panic, and gone to the wrong fish and chip shop at first, and worried when he couldn't find us . . .

We stopped near the Morris Minor and the jeep, those dreadful flashing red lights that hurt your eyes, and a traffic officer squatting outside our car and wanting all sorts of details from Andy—names, addresses, age. Just why we'd been left behind was thankfully not asked. Andy could tell them about Keith, but we knew nothing about Vicki when it came to the point, other than her first name. I sat zonked in the front of Dad's car, staring fascinated at the two mangled cars, imagination running riot with mangled bodies, pity for Vicki. How badly hurt were they?

And yes, there was more than a touch of self-righteousness. If I hadn't . . . if Andy hadn't . . . When the questions had finished and Dad started us on the homeward journey, Andy's hand sought mine from the back seat and held it very tightly all the way back to his place.

Apart from weeping on Mum's shoulder when we got home, I never told anyone. Neither did Andy, in fact I don't think he told his parents at all. Dad somehow found out the next day which hospital they were in. Andy went to see Keith's mother, but she was at the hospital and when he finally got her on the phone she could hardly put two words together. The report in the paper on Monday morning confirmed that two teenagers thrown from a car on the Helensville highway after a two-car collision early Saturday night were in a stable condition in hospital. The seventeen-year-old boy had sustained two broken legs and multiple cuts, the sixteen-year-old girl thrown through the windscreen had facial injuries and a broken arm. The driver of the other car, a local farmer, was in a comfortable condition with cuts and abrasions.

In my family, only Jamie saw the picture of the two cars and put two and two together. After his first few awkward questions, he was told as little as possible and sworn to secrecy. Gran fussed over me even more than usual, although it should have been the other way around because we all knew she wasn't particularly well.

Mum commented that it would have made a nice little story for the papers, my escape. I fear I was very rude, both about her even thinking such a thought, and about reporters who would probably have agreed.

I'd decided, even before Andy hinted when he rang the day after, not to go anywhere near Keith in hospital. The time would come, he said. Right now Keith was a pretty mixed-up lad, with his legs in traction and inclined to blame the farmer in his jeep and, slightly, me and Vicki, for what had happened. Me? Well, you'd upset him, hadn't you, being rude about his driving, and the row with Vicki had been going on for days. Maybe one day he'd appreciate a visit. Well, I said, I'll send a note, just saying I'm sorry he was hurt and get better soon. If he thinks I'm trying to score a point he's stupider than I thought.

I cycled over to the hospital to see Vicki after school, or rather what I could see of her face. Those huge eyes peered at me with a strange expression, not hostile, rather, dare I say, the same look as in the eyes of the little third formers who follow me around. Neither of us could say much—she because of the bandages, and me because I hate hospitals. I just didn't know *what* to say, and I couldn't stop wondering what she looked like behind the bandages. Everything I tried sounded wrong. After a few false starts, I took her hand, and then a nurse stopped at the end of the bed. My face must have been all doom and gloom for she said, 'Not as bad as it looks, fortunately. One of the luckier ones. She'll be OK, there'll be a scar or two across her forehead, which her hair will hide.'

Vicki was still holding my hand. 'I wish,' she said. 'What?' I said leaning over to hear. '. . . I had your . . .', 'Shush,' I said. I had a nasty feeling she was going to say something like courage or confidence or stuff like that. 'I'm just pig-headed. Look after Number One, I do.' After a pause she said, 'Keith had some flowers sent.' I followed her eyes to a magnificent heap of roses, carnations, the works. It was a nice way to say sorry, despite that nonsense he'd told Andy, which I certainly wasn't going to pass on. Spoil someone's face for life, even just a scar hidden by hair; save your own face with your mates. If she still liked him, after this, good luck to her. One of these days he might grow up. Driving-wise, he might not.

There are strange things going on around me. I am aware of some late-night talks between Mum and Dad, and I overheard enough one night to guess they were arguing about Gran, and, although I couldn't see the connection, an overdraft out of control. But Mum has these great ears too, and when she heard the wooden floor creak as I went past on my way to the bathroom the voices stopped.

Gran herself never stops—working or telling everyone how well she is. Then why do I notice one day how thin her arms are sticking out from the cardigan?

Back at school I am sufficiently subdued after the Helensville trip for Julia to ask if I'm OK, I seem pretty quiet these days, and how's my leg. 'Good, good,' I say, referring only to the leg that was almost back to normal size with careful nursing by Mr Jack and his physio friend. But I feel Julia is hiding something, just like I am hiding Helensville. All these secrets are getting on my nerves.

I didn't even hear from Andy for a couple of weeks. I knew he was working hard for end-of-term exams, but it was more than that. He'd withdrawn, as I knew I had. Then there was a phone call one night and an invitation to meet at the American milk bar after school.

'Very daring of you. My parents aren't all that keen . . .'

'I need a break. I need to see you, without family, kids. Please.'

'Five o'clock. I've got rehearsal till then.'

When I hitched my bike to the lamp-post outside, he was already waiting at one of the tables. We ordered Rangitoto Special sundaes and as he brought them over to the table I noticed he was limping himself.

'What's up with the leg?'

'Hamstring. At the weekend.'

'Rugby game?'

'Yes.'

'I'm sorry. Not a good year for legs.'

He had the grace to smile as he said, 'Bit of a relief really. I wasn't going to make the rep trials anyway, but D-D- the old man wouldn't believe that. And he's on my back about swot, exam marks . . .'

I nodded. There was an awkward silence as we both dug through the scarlet sauce into the ice-cream below. 'Could've been worse,' I said pointedly.

'I very nearly didn't get out of the car that night . . .' he said.

'I know.'

'It was only your leg that . . .'

'Was it?'

'You were being so damn righteous. You know, if nothing had happened, Keith would never have let me forget it.'

'If you say so. I wouldn't know. I don't know what goes on between males, except that it seems pretty weird sometimes. All that boloney about it being everyone else's fault but his . . .'

120

'What I'm trying to say, if you'll only let me get a word in edgeways, is . . . I owe you some thanks.'

After a bit, I said, 'Would you really have left me there, if I hadn't had a bum leg, on the side of the road, miles from anywhere?'

'I was pretty angry with you. You put me in an impossible situation.'

'I was angry too, mate. Encouraging him into the pub . . .'

'Not true.'

'You didn't stop him. You didn't say a damn thing.'

'What did you expect me to do. T-take his car keys away?'

'Why not?'

'He drives no worse . . .'

'That *can't* be true. Two broken legs, one girlfriend scarred for life and I don't know about the farmer, how he's getting on. Two wrecked cars.'

Andy was silent.

'He doesn't seem like your type at all.'

'Meaning?'

'Girls at school say he's wild, moody. And randy. Doesn't like it when anyone objects.'

'That figures, up to a point. Do they also say that his father walked out two years ago with a secretary seventeen years younger. That his mum has to work full-time, that his younger sister is a mongol, expensively looked after in some home, and the middle one a real handful, climbing out of windows at night to go to dances?'

I took refuge in my sundae. 'No.'

'He's going to design the most graceful, slender

bridges ever built, his words, true. He's got a scrap-book of every stage of the harbour bridge being built. Every weekend, five, six, years, taking pictures. Plays the guitar, belongs to the CND, worries his head silly about bombs . . .'

An interesting guy, under the tough Marlon Brando exterior.

'He was showing off that night. He'd had a row with Vicki.'

'I guessed.'

'You were famous. And taller than him.'

'So somehow I'm . . .'

'No, of course not. I didn't mean that, Alex.'

He looked so wretched that I took pity. 'No. Well, how's he getting on?'

'Comes out of hospital next week. Pity about the rep team. He'll still beat us all in the scholarship exam, though, with no work,' he said ruefully.

Catch a falling star, put it in your pocket,
Keep it for a rainy day . . .

Some noisy chewing-gum types in jeans and leather jackets had come in and started up the juke box.

'Aren't people . . . amazing . . . what they do, what they've done. You never know, do you, what goes on.' I licked the last of the sauce off the spoon. 'I'm full!'

'Disgusting. You've got a bit of weight aboard, Alex.'

'Come on—I've only been back training a couple of weeks. And pretty gentle at that.'

'You mean two miles instead of four.'

'Not even that. And no ballet or hockey.' Alex, you're at it again. Playing it all down when you know you're up to your eyebrows.

'So what else have you got on?'

'School C. Piano exam in November. Oh, and *Wizard.*'

'What wizard?'

'Didn't I tell you. I'm the stupid Tinman, with my face all silver. Our annual production. The usual shambles.'

'And A. A. in full cry, yet again. I don't know how you find the time.'

'You sound like my grandmother.'

'Strange choice of show for a girls' school, isn't it?'

'You haven't heard Miss Macrae who's producing it. She has a real thing about musicals, which she says are the most exciting development in popular theatre since Shakespeare. Shows that run for years and then films, she says, that give pleasure to millions. She's played us lots of recordings—*West Side Story, My Fair Lady, Salad Days, Gigi, Guys 'n' Dolls*, even *The Wizard of Oz* . . . What we're doing is a watered down version of the film. "If I only had a heart" . . . my song.'

'Sure I'll come, silver girl. It'll suit you.'

He meant all my silver medals. 'Beast.'

I am! I can, Andy! I'm closing the gap.

*Breathing each stroke now, because I've no breath
left for anything else.*

*Too late? Thrown away at the turn, with that
feeble push-off?*

*But I'm feeling good, strong. I'm riding up over
my bow wave. One race in five, perhaps, comes this
surge, this incredible sensation that I'm being pulled,
propelled through the water by some invisible force,
not just my own muscles.*

*I'm in overdrive, relentless. Pain has gone. I know
I can do it now. I'm almost flying.*

*Coming to get you, Maggie Benton. This'll teach
you, Maggie Benton, bringing coaches in from Australia for special coaching all to yourself and not
telling anyone. Only that you'd gone out of town to
train for the week before the nationals. It took a few
days for the grapevine to shake out the news that the
coach you'd had in Queensland last August holidays
just happened to be in the same place the same week.
Funny that.*

I hate to spoil your little plans, Mrs Benton, but

Aussie coaches or not, Maggie's not going to win this race. You can spend all the money you like, but when we get in the pool we're all equal.

You can't blame your equipment like most other sports, or the weather, or being put off by someone screaming instructions from the sideline. There's just your body and a whole lot of water to get through faster than any other body. Your body, and your will, against hers.

You're not level yet, Alex. She's holding you off. She's not beaten yet. Oh, what's twenty seconds of agony after what you've been through in the last eight months? Don't chuck it away . . .

Andy, I hear you. But I'm hurting like hell . . .

8

If Andy, or my family, or Mr Jack, or the teachers at school all thought that, at last, Alex had settled into some sort of reasonable routine, they were being successfully fooled, as intended. End-of-term meant exams, the *Wizard* in the last week. My early morning three miles, twice-weekly calisthenics, daily weights and minimal piano practice were going on as well. I was beginning to wonder myself how I had ever fitted in hockey and ballet.

Winter storms raged as I cycled hither and yon. After the initial pleasure of being back in the water, training had quickly become a grind, especially with a lot of arms-only stuff while the leg got stronger. Maggie and I ploughed up and down on opposite sides of the indoor pool over in town, where there'd been that first race all those years ago. The warm salt water, heavily chlorinated, was still a problem there. Goggles always filled up with water and were not an answer. We tried castor oil, all sorts of chemists' potions, but how could anything work when it just got washed out? It took all my courage to dive into the water each morning, knowing that after a length my eyes would be stinging like after some nasty medieval torture. We had over two months of this, until the freshwater Olympic Pool opened in October.

I knew I was slipping behind in class. I could hardly see my books, let alone a blackboard, for the first part of each morning. All lunch hours and even study periods were *Wizard* rehearsals. Exams loomed, and the only time I had for extra work was during rehearsals when I wasn't needed (which wasn't often: Tinman didn't say all that much, but was on stage a lot) or late at night. A towel along the bottom of my door hid the strip of light sometimes until one or two in the morning.

Only the daily escape into the merry old land of Oz kept me sane. On stage I could forget everything: the very word Helensville, the exams, training, red-hot eyes, the silly leg, which still ached occasionally. But not Andy, even though I hadn't seen him for weeks because he was in the middle of exams; I thought about him *all* the time between phone calls with a sort of exquisite ache. If that's what falling in love feels like, then I'd fallen.

Even with the *Wizard* I knew I was skating on thin ice. I'd learnt my lines in a hurry and at dress rehearsal still needed three prompts, less than some, but in my book inexcusable. And that morning I'd woken from a nightmare where, fully-dressed as Tinman I'd spent the half hour before curtain-up frantically trying to cram the lines into my head, knowing that I'd never do it and would be left standing speechless and humiliated.

Backstage before the first night was the usual shambles. Fathers still hammering scenery, third-former Munchkins everywhere, violinists tuning up, flutes piping, Miss Macrae's voice echoing around the classrooms, which had been turned into dressing-rooms, squads of mothers and teachers helping with make-up. I was a nervous gibbering wreck, again unusual for me.

Inside the costume (silver lamé breeches and shirt, silver socks, sandshoes and gloves, breastplate of cardboard painted silver) and watching my face disappear, I wondered, and not for the first time, what the hell I was doing here.

'Alex, you look superb,' Miss Macrae was booming at me, with various Munchkins staring awestruck at her handiwork. I had just put the helmet, shaped like a funnel, on top of it all. My face was silver with eyes heavily rimmed in black, Charlie Chaplin style, two dinky black eyebrows like little boomerangs, and a red rosebud mouth. My nose was tipped in black and I had some rivets along my jawline. Almost a clown face. I had vanished, without trace. Towering above the Dorothy, who was a third former, and the pint-sized Lion, and Janice equally unrecognizable as the Scarecrow, I felt like some bizarre statue, a metallic lighthouse with legs. What *am* I doing here?

I don't remember much of the first night. The land of Oz must have worked its magic. The ability I knew I had (and indeed counted on) to rise to the occasion, along with native cunning—and a little bit of luck— got me through. Young Dorothy sang like an angel, almost as beautifully as Judy Garland. My songs passed in a daze, the audience loved the tiny Lion with her deep voice, and the witches, green-faced and grotesque, brought the house down. Through the curtain calls and cries of great, marvellous after the final curtain, stumbling through to the classroom and wiping my face clean, it still felt dream-like. Andy was out there somewhere; but it didn't seem to matter one way or the other.

I dressed slowly, apart from the others, saying little, knowing I looked pale with heavy rings under my eyes, which no amount of cold cream could remove. Was it vanity or self-protection that an echo from another dressing-room had made me choose a very frilly, feminine blouse?

In the corridor outside, I found Andy, smart in tweed sports coat and polo neck. The object too of much giggling and heavy breathing from passing third formers, as well they might.

'Alex, was that really you? Splendid stuff.'

'I don't remember much.' I might have looked wan, but inside, seeing him, I was tingling all over.

'I didn't know you could sing, too.'

'Neither did I. Take me home, please.'

'Aren't your family here?'

'I wouldn't let them come tonight. Tomorrow.' Around us swarmed Munchkins, in street clothes but flaunting their make-up proudly. 'Get me out of here.'

Going home, I could barely speak. Andy chattered on about the show, full of enthusiasm. Outside the house, I could only sit limply when he leaned across and with cool fingers traced the outlines of my face, my pointy chin, hairline greasy with cold cream; hardly romantic.

'A very special girl.'

'No.'

'Yes. Fragile, for all her apparent strength. Needs tender loving care.' He leaned across and kissed me gently. 'Go get some sleep, sweet maid.'

Weak at the knees, I got slowly out of the car. 'You're not going training in the morning,' he stated.

'Yes, I am.'

'My God, Alex, give yourself . . .'

I was half-way up the drive. 'I have to.'

'According to who . . .'

'Me. Don't spoil it Andy. Goodnight, thanks for coming.'

Dad had other thoughts. I slept through the alarm and he didn't stir me. I woke, with a dreadful taste in my mouth, at eight thirty. Dad and the others had already gone, and Mum and Gran were standing either side of the washing machine feeding clothes through the wringer, up to their elbows in suds.

'Why didn't you wake me? I'll be late for school.'

'I think not,' said Mum quietly. 'Porridge in pot, lunch on bench, clean shirt in your room, twenty minutes in hand.' As I stared at her, stupid with sleep, she added, 'Mr Jack agreed. You need sleep more than training this week.'

It was a Jack-up. Ha! I was furious. How dare they decide for me. I stomped off to my room to get dressed. In the mirror I saw two bags under a pair of eyes, closely followed by A. Archer, Tinman Extraordinaire. The very thought of tonight, and tomorrow night, and the last night, made my blood run cold.

At school, those who'd seen the show were complimentary. Still in my dream-like state, I survived the next two nights. I even survived with my family there, but knowing that I sang and spoke my lines without much conviction, not up to Miss Macrae's expectations. Before bed the night they came, I had a heavy argument with Dad about training, him trying to be logical, understanding and so on, but ending with him flatly refusing to wake me or take me, actually forbidding me to go training until the show was over. I knew in my bones he was right. I was pretty near some sort of flash-point.

Andy rang before breakfast on Friday to see how the show was going. He'd finished his exams and, with holidays about to start, was feeling like celebrating.

'I'm coming tonight,' he said.

'You can't. You haven't got a ticket.' Why was I so reluctant for him to be there?

'I'll get one at the door.'

'It's the last night, sold out.'

'Then I'll hang around outside. There's sure to be a single seat or standing room somewhere. Afterwards we'll do something special, how's that?'

Over-ruled, I was silent. I'd got through three nights, but I was full of foreboding about the fourth.

'Alex, you still there?'

'Sort of. See you.' I put the phone down, and went along to breakfast. There was a funny sort of atmosphere in there too.

'Where's Gran?'

'Not feeling too good. She's staying in bed today,' said Mum. 'Jamie, take this tray in to her, will you?'

'I'll go,' I said, earning a most weird look from Jamie. Gran was propped up in bed drinking tea, surrounded by piles of unfinished baby dresses. She looked about seven hundred years old.

'You shouldn't be running around after me. You look so tired, Alex.'

'Don't talk rot, Gran. Here's some breakfast. Mum says you've got to stay in bed.'

Surprisingly, she didn't protest.

'What's wrong with Gran?' I said to Mum.

'She needs a rest.'

'You should ask,' said Jamie.

'Meaning?'

'Nothing.' Breakfast passed, the usual grizzlings about who was drying the dishes. Mum seemed pre-occupied, I gave her a hand with the lunches. Dad left earlier than usual.

'Try to get a sleep after school,' Mum said.

'I can't sleep in the day.'

Mum slammed down the bread knife. 'God help me, I'm surrounded by obstinate women. I've practically had to chain Gran into her bed. And you walk around looking like a zombie, but you're above sleeping.'

Such explosions were rare. 'OK, OK. I'll have a rest.'

'Poor little Alex,' said Jamie nastily from the sink. 'Never lifts a finger. So who's in bed with overwork, trying to earn money to pay for all her lessons and being in sport and shows and trips and things . . .'

'Jamie,' shouted Mum, an even rarer event. 'You will stop immediately.' Usually it would have been me first in the debate, but this time I was too weary and too thunderstruck to do anything other than gape at Jamie. I was to blame for Gran in bed, getting so thin? Is that where all the money she earned went? Rows between Mum and Dad? An overdraft out of control?

I took a silent ten seconds or so to gather up my sandwiches, then I walked out of the kitchen, aware that Mum was trying to regain control of herself, and Jamie was probably both scared and pleased at what he'd said. I sank on my bed, and saw Mum's figure in the doorway through tears.

'Why did he say that? How would he know anything about it?'

Mum sighed. 'Dad and I had a row last night while you were at school, about money as usual. I can only assume he heard a bit, behind the door. We should have driven off somewhere in the car and had it out . . .'

'So it's true?'

'Only partly. The money Gran earns from her dresses helps pay for your lessons, coaching fees. Jamie's too, and there'll be extra things for the others as they get older. We've always wanted you to have every oppor . . .'

'Why didn't you tell me? She slaves away out there . . .'

'Gran's a very proud little lady, Alex. Her whole life has been family, since Dad died, helping me, helping us. She's made of stern stuff. Napier in the 1920s, raising children through the Depression, the earthquake, it was a pretty hard road if your husband's shop fell down, *and* he took to drink.'

Dad? My grandfather? You never knew, did you?

'I'm going out to see her.'

'Alex, if you really want to help her, you'll say nothing about money, or her working herself to a standstill, so you can swim . . .'

'It all seems so . . . so, pointless, now.'

'What does?'

'Just trying to swim faster than Maggie, when Gran looks like she does out there. If that's . . .'

'I told you. She's as tough as old boots. Two days in bed, she'll be back at her sewing machine and nothing I, you or anyone can do will change that. So, we've got to use very subtle methods to lighten her load.'

'Like me giving up swimming.'

'That would be the worst thing. Her reward is your success, your achievements. She just loved the show last night. When you win the nationals, she'll be in seventh heaven knowing that in her own way she's helped you get to Rome.'

When, she said, not if. 'Thanks, Mum,' I said, giving her a big hug. 'Can I go and see her now?'

'Just . . . belonging, is all she needs. I couldn't manage without her—well, I could, lots do. But she knows what it means to me, her help . . . And please don't say anything to Jamie.'

Gran had not touched her breakfast. Sleeping, she looked only about two hundred years old. I bent down and kissed her cheekbone, which was the least lined part of her face. 'Sleep well.' She grunted, her eyelids moved. 'See you after school, Gran.'

Despite my own extra hours' sleep each morning, by mid-morning I was feeling so tired, and still upset by what I'd heard, I was almost light-headed. I saw Miss Macrae looking at me in assembly; later she bailed me up in the corridor. Was I all right, and then some nice stuff about my stage presence, comic timing and generosity to my fellow performers. I hardly knew what she was talking about. Was it obvious I was on a tightrope?

There was no understudy, therefore no escape from tonight. The Lion, Daphne, and Scarecrow, Janice, were both sixth formers, gaily riding the wave of success and (unknown to me) anticipating some high-jinks traditional on the last night. Yet even they, when I walked into our dressing-room that evening, took one look at me and burst forth.

'You OK?'

'You sick or something? You look awful!'

'Thanks, pals, for those heart-warming words of encouragement. Guaranteed to make a girl feel just fine.'

Julia was in our room too, in her green Emerald City garb, looking at me critically as I started to undress. Not the frilly blouse tonight; I had more important things to worry about.

'Stop gawking at me, Julia. I'm fine.'

She made a doubtful face, but didn't say anything. As I put on the silver socks, breeches, shirt, there

135

was a lot of chat. Clearly the others were out to enjoy this last performance. I'd just be glad to get it over.

'My God, look at you.' One of the witches came through the door. If her green make-up had been bizarre on previous nights, now she looked positively macabre. The atmosphere of last night recklessness made me even more determined to get through the show unscathed. I was enough of an idiot in my silver clown face, without making it worse. Mercifully, I did not have to insist that only Miss Macrae do my make-up. Skilfully, professionally, even soothingly, her fingers smoothed on the silver goo (imported especially, guaranteed non-toxic), obliterating the dark shadows. I was almost beginning to like hiding inside this Tinman.

The Kansas farm, Munchkinland and Scarecrow's song came and went. Janice was in top form. Watching in the wings as my scene drew closer, I put the two halves of the breastplate on and got one of the chorus to tie the bows holding it together. I heard a snort and snigger behind me, and titters, which must have been audible to the audience. I turned around.

'What is it?' I mouthed.

Eyes are all I remember, glinting with malice.

The curtain had closed on the witches. I had about ten seconds of music to get into position. I stormed on to the stage, where Dorothy and Scarecrow were standing ready.

'What is wrong with me?' I demanded.

They looked at me blankly.

'Tell me, otherwise I'll walk right off this stage, now, and not come back.'

In the pit outside, the orchestra faded out. The stage manager was frantically signalling to the curtain operator not to pull the curtains. The audience shuffled in the silence.

'Tell me, or I leave.'

But I was too late. The curtain had begun to open. I had two seconds to decide: leave or continue and take the consequences. Four lines into the scene, they were supposed to discover me behind a bush. I just couldn't leave them there on the stage, looking silly. I leapt into my rigid, rusted-up Tinman position on the side of the stage.

Janice began the scene, outwardly fine but eyes wary. By now my adrenaline was flowing nicely. I decided, whatever was on my back, I'd act them all off the stage. I heard my voice calling for oil in a heavy Texas accent. I deliberately manoeuvered Janice upstage so that she could see my back. When I turned to look at her, I had the satisfaction of seeing that behind her Scarecrow make-up she was nearly beside herself. Serve you right, I thought, unfairly no doubt. Little Dorothy was wide-eyed, more terrified than amused, clearly wondering what was going to happen next.

I turned my song into a soft shoe number, putting in all sorts of nimble steps, totally out of character, and belted out the final phrases in a voice to rival Ethel Merman, 'If I on-lee-had-a-HEART.' Then with my arms outstretched for the final note, a long high E, I swung around and presented the audience with my back.

The laughter and clapping went on for so long that

I was obliged to turn around and follow Miss Codlin's lead to sing the song again. Even the orchestra, who'd sat through umpteen boring rehearsals, was nearly falling off its collective seats. Before that, however, I muttered to Janice under the applause what the hell they were laughing at.

'You'd rather not . . .'

'Tell me,' I hissed.

'Campbell's Soup,' she muttered. 'Made in Hong Kong. In red paint.' In the wings delighted faces watched in tiers.

Not so funny, I thought sourly. Have you ever tried to keep a straight face when all about you have completely lost their cool? I suppose professional actors have to be able to do it. I now decided to see if I could, too. As I heard the orchestra begin the four-bar intro, I thought, I'll show you. So I belted out the song again, giving the Codlin Moth a hard time, and made up a quite bizarre little dance, with comic *pas de chat* and silly arabesques. As the *coup de grâce* I did an almighty jump and finished with the splits. Ever seen a Tinman do the splits? No? This one shouldn't have either because getting to my feet again I felt a distinct pull in my leg.

It was unforgivable, really. Dorothy and Janice stood there bent double, the audience by this time laughing with them, as one does when actors have got the giggles. I stood snapped rigid into my Tinman pose, while all hell broke loose. The longer I stood, the more they laughed. It became a test, to see if they could break me. But swimmers spend hours every day staring at the bottom of a pool, switched off, thinking of nothing in particular. After a while, I was actually enjoying the control I found I had.

Thank God my family aren't here. Andy—oh shit!

From the wings, I heard a stage whisper, Miss Macrae, 'Get on with the scene, Dorothy.' Eventually she did, with me still the po-faced injured party. The audience seemed to find everything I said hilarious. I tried out an English accent, then broad Aussie and broader Scots. When the Munchkins came on they were supposed to be all nervous about the hazards of the journey to the Land of Oz but the scene was ruined. When we finally got on to the Yellow Brick Road, my nerve was beginning to go, but I was up to my silver neck in it now. We swung through that number like we never swung before. It was written as a trio with chorus, but it became my dance. This time I was a tipsy marching girl. The Munchkins didn't have a show.

I have to hand it to Miss Macrae. She'd already decided there'd be an interval and sent a message to the Codlin Moth. As I stood gasping behind the closed curtain, hearing the torrent of applause, I knew Miss Macrae, who'd played Joan of Arc on the London stage, could have destroyed me for ever. But she merely held back the surge of excitement with a raised hand and said quietly, 'Ten minutes' interval, girls, to calm down a little.'

I felt a hand take mine. Although Miss Macrae had not finished talking, Julia led me offstage through rows of grinning teeth and into the classroom. She sat me on a chair, knelt and undid the fastenings of the breastplate.

It was worse even than Campbell's Soup and Made in Hong Kong. Painted in large black letters, a heart with an arrow stuck through it said A LOVES A. Where my bottom would have been was a card, stuck on crudely with chewing gum. I remember someone pressing up against me in the wings. This one read HANDLE WITH CARE.

I swear the flush was visible through the silver. With just a little fight left in me before I crawled into my hole, I snatched the breastplate from Julia and bent it across my knee. Then I hurled it into a corner.

'Take that bloody thing away, burn it or do any damn thing you like with it, but piss off, all of you . . .'—this for the benefit of a few faces that had appeared at the door. 'Leave me alone. I'm going home.'

'Alex.'

The steely voice boomed through my rage.

'And you can stick your wizard . . .'

'Alex, sit down, please.'

Deflated and shaking, I sat. I had the wrong costume on, I was the Scarecrow minus all his stuffing. There was an ominous pause while Miss Macrae walked into the room. People have been expelled for swearing at teachers.

'Before a race, I'm sure you do this, Alex. Singers also, musicians. Hands on diaphragm, deep breaths, feel that rib cage expand, shoulders steady.'

The Tinman had rusted up for ever.

'Alex, ten deep breaths, with me. One, two, three . . .' I matched her rhythm. 'Good, now ten more.'

She stood behind me and expertly massaged my shoulders. And I, traitor that I was, thought she's enjoying this, a chance at last to touch me. But her strong fingers were easing away the tension.

'So tight! Now listen to me, Alex, you've got a performance to finish . . .'

I jumped like a cat. 'No.'

'Relax, let yourself go.' Her fingers both hurt and eased me. 'You have an obligation, mainly to yourself but also to the rest of us . . .'

'I can't.'

'I believe you can.'

I looked up. In the mirror was this unlikely pair, the silver clown with staring glazed black eyes, the middle-aged woman with short grey hair above. It wasn't me in there, it was someone else. I was at home, in bed.

'How could they?'

'It wasn't only you.'

'Why me?'

'You were just the first, believe me. Lion had a pair of wings sewn into her costume, and for Scarecrow, well, I shudder to think what they were going to do with a string of sausages. Intestines, possibly. Our Wizard had secreted about her person, under her cape, a dead fish, a golf umbrella and a tiny third former dressed as a chicken. Highly unprofessional and irresponsible. I shall find out who was involved.'

'Too late now. I've ruined everything . . .'

'No, you haven't.' She stopped massaging and pulled up a chair to sit very close to me. 'Alex, you're very talented . . .'

'No,' I cried. 'It's all a lie, I fail, every time.'

'Nine out of ten professional actors could not have survived on that stage tonight. Your control was quite breath-taking. And that was a very funny dance. Will you believe me when I say it was brilliant, I haven't laughed so much for a long time. If I didn't personally think that law, court work, or maybe politics, was the most suitable career for your undoubted gifts once you've got all that sport out of your system, I should recommend that you trained for the stage. Despite your height, or even carrying your height to your advantage.'

'That wasn't me,' I muttered.

'Oh yes it was.' She smiled. 'You, with your inhibitions loosened by anger and defiance and embarrassment. Most people need booze to enjoy themselves quite as much as that in public. Actors need years of experience. Women find it particularly hard. There's a reluctance to take the risk of making a fool of yourself.'

I was silent. Enjoy myself? Had I? Oh, yes, I'd ridden that wave of audience approval with guns blazing.

'I did make a fool of myself, didn't I?'

'Look at me, Alex. The answer is no. You played to the gallery, you carried it off superbly. Now, I'm asking you to use that discipline, that control I've just seen, to finish the show. There'll be no more pranks.'

Something in my eyes must have signalled, I'll try.

'Good girl.' She stood up, hands on my shoulders, almost as though trying to knead her will, her strength and her experience into me. 'The audience will expect more of the same. Don't get rattled. Just play it as we rehearsed. They'll soon settle down.'

Brisk, booming voice again. 'Janice, get the cast on stage for me. Alex, you sit quietly for a few minutes.'

'No, I'm coming.' I saw a smile before she left. Julia had moved across to pick up my battered armour. 'Not much we can do about this, Alex,' she said, trying to flatten out the cracks. 'You'll just have to keep your front to the audience.'

That won't be difficult, I thought, standing wearily, while Julia tied on the breastplate.

'You'll be fine,' she said. I checked myself in the mirror. I still had the oddest feeling that it was someone else inside that costume, behind the silver mask. 'Come on.'

Keeping to the back, I caught a few curious looks, nudges, and giggles as we assembled behind the curtain. The second act, Miss Macrae announced briskly, was to proceed as rehearsed. Anyone rash enough to try any more pranks on stage would be severely dealt with.

Then it was house lights again, orchestra and back on to the Yellow Brick Road. I was back into my dream-like trance of the previous nights, just going through the motions. After my initial few lines, the audience seemed to sense I'd done my dash and shifted their enjoyment to Daphne's wonderful husky, petrified Lion and later the witches.

Final curtain, speeches, thanks, bouquets, I stood as inconspicuously as my height and a silver face allowed. As soon as it was all over, Julia had my hand again. 'Let's go.' In the dressing-room she started to undress me.

'You'll make a wonderful nurse,' I mumbled. 'But an even better doctor.'

'Hush.' Then harshly to a swarm of excitable people trying to get in through the door, 'Get out all of you. No one's allowed in here for ten minutes except those needing to change.'

'Who said?'

'I said. Alex is not well. Now scram.' I heard the door bang. 'Rabble we can do without.'

I seemed powerless to help myself. I obeyed her orders like a dummy. Stripped to bra and silver breeches, my hair scraped back from the silver mask which looked like one of those Greek tragedy masks on our school Shakespeare books, I surveyed myself in the mirror and began to laugh. It was not a good moment for the swell in the noises from the corridor outside as the door opened and shut, a male voice saying firmly, 'I'm her brother.'

There stood Andy.

Some brother. By now I was laughing fit to bust.

Julia moved first, with a dressing-gown which she slipped around my shoulders.

'She's cold and exhausted,' I heard her say. 'And she's about to have hysterics.'

I roared at my reflection. Ha ha *ha*, ho ho *ho*, the Merry Old Land of Oz, get lost. Hysterics, what's that. The Tinman is cracking up. I scooped up a great dollop of cold cream from a pot and threw it at my face. I rubbed at the silver mask. The stuff went in my eyes, ears, hair, very quickly becoming a nasty molten mess.

'When a man's an empty kettle, he's always on his mettle,' I sang. Another scoop of cold cream. 'And yet I'm torn apart.' I threw the dressing-gown off. '. . . I could be kinda human, If I Only Had a *Heart*.' Ethel Merman again. There was a sinister silence in the corridor now. Were they all listening? Julia and Andy were moving towards me, coming to get me. If I noticed anything at all, it was the expression on Andy's face, aghast, as I spat out what I had to say.

'I'd be tender, I'd be gentle, I'd be awful sentimental—you know what they say, Andy . . . ? Because I always . . . have to be, wind up a male in these charades, they think . . . do you know what they think, they *think* I'm a bit odd, I'm nearly six foot tall and built like a tank, and I've got this funny tenor voice . . . What do you think, Andy? I shouldn't be swimming against proper girls like Maggie, that's what they say. Perhaps I'm a neuter. Isn't there a word, hermaph . . . hermaph . . . Oh, I could be kinda human if I only had a . . .'

Andy had grabbed one sticky hand, Julia the other. My knees buckled as they forced me back on to a chair.

Now I knew they were coming, the tears I'd held back for days and weeks, even months since Maggie's dance. I heard Andy's voice. There was a towel in his hand. 'Alex, sweet maid. Hold her hands, Julia. Alex, please, Alex, let me . . .'

I was draped across the chair, my head thrown back. I felt the tension literally dripping out of me. Fingers were gently wiping my face clean, as soothingly as Miss Macrae had put the stuff on.

'Nearly gone now, Tinman, for ever,' Andy said. Mothers talked like that to their children, soothing away a nightmare, a hurt. I'd done it myself, to various brothers and sisters. 'Nearly gone, rest now.'

If only I could. 'I'm going training in the morning.' If I kept this up, I could train in my own tears.

'We'll see.' Mothers said that too, fobbing off. 'There now. Sit up, Alex . . .'

I looked at myself again. There were still black smudges where my eyes should have been, globs of cold cream in my hair, but mostly I was me again. I wept afresh, on to the shoulder of Andy's nice sports coat.

'We've got to get some clothes on her,' said Julia. 'She's shaking, but whether from cold or . . .'

'He's seen me in bikinis before,' I sniffed. 'Don't be prudish, Julia. And don't talk about me as though I'm not here.'

'I'm not,' Julia began indignantly.

'If you're going to be a doctor, you can't be prudish. Andy here, now he's not going to be a doctor, he's going to sea, aren't you Andy? Funny that, both your parents . . . Julia thinks she's going to have to be a nurse, but that's only her silly father. I think you're very brave, Julia. I can't *stand* the sight of blood.'

'She's away with the fairies,' I heard Julia mutter. 'Do you think we should call a doctor?' How sharp were all my senses, especially my great ears which heard far too much. I heard the door open and shut again.

'Get some clothes on, Alex,' said Miss Macrae brutally. 'Time to go home and sleep. Holidays as of now, three whole weeks, thank God.'

Julia was on hand with shirt, jumper, skirt, shoes.

'I'm very proud of you, Alex,' said Miss Macrae. 'That took courage.'

I could only wail, but I was running out of tears.

Julia said, 'This is her boyfriend, Andy Richmond.'

'Good, you take her home as soon as we can get some clothes on her. Come on, Alex, help yourself. Make a fuss of your girl, Andy. She needs it. We all need reassurance from time to time when we think we've gone off the rails . . .'

I was down to sniffing and snuffling now. I had never felt more totally drained in my life.

'One day when you win a few gold medals, or you're making a name for yourself in court, or whatever you choose to do, I'll think back to tonight. Raw talent, off the leash. You'll remember it too, Alex, and chuckle.'

I wasn't smiling yet. But Andy was.

'Don't laugh at me,' I whispered, pathetically. 'Please, Andy, don't laugh.'

He was staring at me, remembering. 'I wouldn't have believed it possible. If a Hollywood talent scout had been here . . .'

'Don't.'

'Will you listen just for once? Can't you believe I'm so proud of you I could burst? That I stood there at the side and just marvelled? What are you afraid of?'

'It's a female problem,' said Miss Macrae. 'Reluctance to make a fool of herself. I did it, often enough. I know what it takes.'

I looked at her, with her severe grey fringe and tailored suit. She looked more like an off-duty hospital matron.

'I always got the character parts, blacked up for minstrel shows, pantomime horses, Cinderella's ugly sister, Noel Coward revues, lots of ghosts, witches— *Macbeth*, the opera of *Hansel and Gretel*. A riotous version of *The Taming of the Shrew*, in a red wig.'

Katherine the Shrew, Miss Macrae?

'Now, Andy Richmond, take your girl home. Leave all your stuff, Alex. Julia will look after it.'

We went out a side door, to avoid Munchkins and others. Andy treated me like a sick patient coming home from hospital and I wasn't going to protest. Truth to tell, I felt as though I'd been through some kind of storm at sea, washed up, some ordeal by fire, melted down. I also knew I wouldn't be training tomorrow, because I didn't think I'd wake for about three days.

*Some things I do know, Andy. Round about here,
races are won or lost. Maggie, for the first time in
her life, too, is swimming this race to win. Never
mind what the stop-watch says. And she's increased
her stroking rate.*

*I've gained, yet still she holds me off. Half a yard,
a hand? Are my arms that much longer when it
comes to the final lunge for the wall?*

*No, they're not. I've mighty long arms, like an
albatross, a wing span of over two yards, but that's
not long enough.*

*Round about here races are lost, Alex. Oh think
ahead, sweet maid, to the wall, to Rome.*

*That Aussie coach sitting out there with Lady Ben-
ton. He might ask me to join his squad in Queensland
. . . what about a scholarship to an American university . . .*

*Put that in your pipe, Mrs Benton. Oh I'm slip-
ping, I'm slipping, I'm going backwards for Christmas . . .*

*Alex, you're not concentrating. Your stroke rate—
can you move it up a notch?*

9

When Mum puts her foot down, which is not often, it goes down hard. I woke up after two solid days' sleep, getting out of bed only to pee and sit silently at the family table to eat some food. Mum, with Gran back on her feet ('I am *not* staying in there another day, Helena,' I heard her indignant voice) was in no mood for discussion. Messages had been taken, from Julia and Miss Macrae and also Miss Gillies, to see how I was; Alex is fine, thanks, I heard Mum say on the phone, catching up on sleep and going away for a few days. I was? I was about to do what I was told.

'Your father has taken three days off work,' she said quietly after tea on Sunday night, cheese on toast around the fire. We were in for two weeks of school holidays for the brats, three for me. I'd planned on catching up with training, weights, some extra piano practice, and swot, with School Cert only two months away, and miles of notes to revise.

'Why?' Dad never took time off work, even to come to champs and things. He just couldn't. He had two weeks' holiday a year and that was that.

'I've rung up your Auntie Pat. You can use their beach house.'

'Mum, I've got to start *training*.'

'I've already spoken to Mr Jack,' said Dad. 'He

agrees that what you need right now is a complete break. We'll be back Wednesday night. You can start Thursday.'

I thought, I can't stand people organizing my life for me, but I knew a brick wall when I saw one.

'Andy is coming, too,' said Dad.

'*What?*'

'Don't say what, please Alex. I spoke to him yesterday. He's got permission from his parents, provided he brings his books and does four hours a day.'

'Dad!'

'What's the matter? I thought you two got on well.'

'You seem to have me all sorted out.'

'That's right,' said Mum. 'This time we have, and about time. Three days of sea air will do you a power of good.'

'I breathe sea air all the time. Auckland's surrounded by sea . . .'

'You know what I mean, Miss Smarty Alec. Blow away the cobwebs. Go for long walks along the beach, read, sleep. I know your leg's not entirely right yet but . . .'

I had my marching orders.

How can you have two totally opposite feelings about the same thing? I was thrilled down to my boots that Andy was coming—and horrified as well. After last Friday night, I thought I'd never be able to look him in the face again. In the car going home, I'd been like a zombie. I knew it, but just couldn't help myself. I'd muttered to myself, and my head kept falling off my neck.

There'd even been a reception committee waiting: Mum and Dad, apparently alerted by a phone call from school. I was helped out of the car like a cripple. Dad would have carried me inside, but he wasn't a giant and there was, frankly, too much of me.

Everyone was deliberately cheerful, speaking too clearly and a touch too loud. What had happened wasn't directly mentioned.

'Bed for you, Alex,' said Mum. 'Cup of tea, Andy?'

So, after I'd had a shower and washed the remaining smudges off my face, they'd all sat around in my bedroom drinking cups of tea and eating digestive biscuits and talking about the Queen having another baby and Krushchev visiting America and the second rugby test against the British Lions in Wellington. Unreal.

Then I fell asleep, just like that. As I went, I heard Mum saying, 'My poor Alex. I'm afraid some people have to learn the hard way.'

Andy: 'She was very *very* funny . . .'

Mum: 'What happened?'

Andy: 'Well . . .'

I gave a tiny scream, 'Shut up Andy,' but I was out for the count.

We picked Andy up at half past eight on Monday morning, fortunately without getting involved with his parents. I'd climbed out of bed still feeling zonked, and apprehensive about Andy coming. When I saw him, I felt much better; what a fine-looking young man, Gran muttered as she came out with me to the car to say goodbye, and he was too. Three days of him, all to myself!

Dad was like a kid wagging school. I suppose when you have two weeks' leave a year, anything else is a bonus.

'Good weather predicted,' he said. 'South-westerlies, occasional showers, mainly fine. Brought your togs, Andy?'

'I never thought to.'

'Pity. Bracing stuff, August swimming. I grew up only a stone's throw from the beach. We had a thriving life-saving club, swam the year round. Well, a few of us did. I've often wondered if that helped when it came to swimming around in the Atlantic when my ship . . .'

'D-did you serve in the Navy, sir?'

Then they were away, all the way out to the coast, or rather Dad was, pleased to find someone interested in his war-time exploits, being torpedoed in the Atlantic and later missing his ship in Crete or somewhere, and the ship going down with all hands two days later. Of course, Dad didn't know that going to sea was all Andy had ever wanted to do, and Andy didn't know that Dad hardly ever talked about the war, and that he should count himself lucky.

I watched the bungalows slip by, content to sit in the front and let Dad's quiet voice put me to sleep. Andy lent over the back of the seat and gently rubbed the back of my neck. I liked hearing them talk, my two favourite men (not forgetting Mr Jack, of course): men's talk. Andy talked about the Sea Cadets he'd been in at school. He was rather sorry that compulsory military training had been stopped last year and he didn't have to go off and do his three months as a naval trainee.

'Sorry?' said Dad. 'Most young blokes I know . . .'

'It's because I want to go to sea,' said Andy in a rush. 'It's all I've ever wanted.' (So now two people know.) 'But my parents want me to do medicine. I've got to t-tell them soon that I'm not going to.'

After a silence, Dad said, 'Will that be difficult?'

'Very.' I felt the finger rubbing my neck stop, as though it was thinking about the problem. 'That's why I want to get good scholarship marks, then I'm in a strong position to convince them I'll get accepted for officer training. Midshipman cadets go to D-D-England, to Dartmouth Naval College, first.'

You'll be going away, Andy? I couldn't bear it. I will wait for ever. My eyelids and my brain closed down as we started the climb up the hills to the beach and the beach house beyond. I'd not been out to the west coast in years. Perhaps this whole junket wasn't such a bad idea after all.

Three days suspended in time. The house was a very small wooden box snuggling up against the hillside, about two hundred yards back from the beach. There were two rooms. One had four bunks, four lumpy pillows, a wooden chest of drawers, that's all. We hung our coats on hooks behind the door. The other room had a wood-burning stove, an enamel sink, some very plain cupboards, a worn table and rickety chairs. Battered tin billies, a frypan that had seen better days, crockery and eating utensils that might have belonged to some old great-aunt, circa 1890. Two 'Beautiful New Zealand' calendars (1953, 1956), two armchairs, fishing gear stacked in a corner and some horrible curtains completed the decor. There was no telephone and no electricity. Water came from a large tin tank beside the house, and the toilet was a long drop in a tiny outhouse twenty yards away.

Dad was rather rude about his sister, Pat, my aunt. 'Married into all that money. Obvious they haven't spent much of it here.'

'I like it as it is,' I said. It was true. I really liked the plain wooden walls and the kerosene lamps flickering away at night. We lit the wood stove late each afternoon and by tea-time it was as warm as toast. Dad did all the cooking: sausages and fried eggs on Monday night, shepherd's pie on Tuesday.

Andy tried, mainly in the early mornings while I was still asleep, but he didn't get much work done. Dad said he, for one, was happy pottering, and might do a spot of fishing later, so Andy and I went for long meandering walks along the beach. There was hardly anyone around, fishermen casting with long lines from the rocks near the car-park, a few like us, just walking, kids scrambling up and jumping down the high dunes of black sand.

On our last day, we soon left them all behind, walking slowly, barefoot through the shallows, kicking at the froth and feeling the suction around our ankles as the waves were pulled back into the ocean. My leg gave me no trouble. Ahead of us the mighty beach swept in a clear curve until it disappeared into the mist. And offshore the surf rolled and broke against a hard blue sky. Hundreds of miles to Australia, thousands to anywhere else.

If Andy was thinking how small my worries were against that seascape, he was right. I could feel myself unwinding.

We found a sheltered crater in amongst the black dunes and sat down for the lunch we'd put together, Marmite sandwiches, cheese, a carrot each, some biscuits Mum had sent with us, a thermos of tea.

As he munched, Andy smiled.

'What's the joke?'

'I was just thinking . . . you won't like this . . . of you on that stage.'

I was already on my feet, brushing the crumbs off my jeans and packing up the thermos.

'You'd better get this straight, Andy Richmond. You mention *The Wizard of Oz* ever again and I'll . . .'

'What? Refuse to see me?'

'Yep.'

'You wouldn't do that. I'm the best friend you've got.'

'That doesn't mean you can keep on teasing and hurting me any old time you want.'

'It means', he said, grabbing my wrist and pulling me towards him, 'I'm going to kiss you like this and not even the famous Alexandra is going to protest.'

How could I, anyway. My legs had given way beneath me and we'd fallen into the sand. I was underneath, helpless, loving it.

When we'd both run out of breath, he said, 'There, Alexandra, now kiss me back.'

One thing led to another and with anyone less strong, I might well have gone, as my older classmates at school so delicately put it, the whole hog. But Andy had firm views about some things and this was one of them. I suppose I did, too, when it came to the point. So we went only half-way.

Pity really, because the sensation of wind against my bare breast and Andy kissing it softly was almost too much for me.

'I want to ask you something,' he said.

'Fire away.'

'If you'd rather not . . .'

'Try me.' He hadn't shaved this morning, and his chin was rough, like sandpaper, a cat's tongue.

'Do you remember saying, after the show, that last night when you were . . . upset . . . you said, people are saying you're odd. Being tall, and good at sport, and you, quote, "always have male roles in these charades" . . .'

After a long while, I said, 'Did I say that?'.

'Something like.'

'Hmmm. Do you remember Maggie's dance? That's what I overheard in the Ladies'. Some little cat and her friend. A friend at her school, quote, "says it's no coincidence she always winds up a male in school shows," unquote. And "she's always hugging girls, and giving her very good friend Julia back rubs" . . .'

'No wonder you came out pink.'

'Do you blame me? Julia's asthmatic, you know that. What am I supposed to do, never touch her when a massage seems to ease it?'

He had pulled back my bush shirt further and was stroking the other breast as well.

'Boys get it, too,' he said. 'Anyone who's not your average guy. Show an interest in music, theatre, smart clothes, poetry, art—you're suspect. Even hockey or soccer is unmanly. If you wanted to be an interior designer, or a ballet d-dancer or a hair-dresser—you'd be called a *girl*, absolutely beyond the pale. Real men play footie, or watch it, and prop up the bar until six. Then they go home and listen to the radio to find out how much they've lost on the horses, swear at their kids and beat up their wives.'

'You like jazz and Gershwin and Noel Coward . . .'

'I keep that very quiet. And I play in the First Fifteen, which puts me beyond suspicion. Anyway, I thought it might help, well, to know you're not alone in this. Others get knocked too, people who are different and successful. You gotta get cut down to size. I've a teacher at school, a real larger-than-life Englishman, who says it's a New Zealand national pastime.'

'It's worse still for girls. No one's really expected to have great ambitions. Nearly all my class are going to do nursing or teaching or secretarial work, travel a bit, catch a husband and disappear for ever into the suburbs.'

'What about Julia? She's going to do medicine, you said.'

'Her father says he can't afford to put her through university, as well as two brothers. She'll end up nursing, you'll see. Girls are expendable in the end. The Head at school says it wasn't always like this, girls being talked out of careers, out of higher education. At least *you* are encouraged, great things are expected, great scholarship marks. At our school they won't even let the Upper Sixth girls *sit*. Only a few people are encouraging me: Mum and Dad, some of the teachers at school.'

'I am.'

'OK, you. The rest think I'm crazy to want to do law. And then people say, because you want a proper career so that you're independent and you happen to be tall and have broad shoulders and can swim a bit, that you're not feminine. Career girls are hard, selfish and not true women.'

'I wish you'd told me at the time why . . .'

'Not likely! I wouldn't have told anyone, ever, except for . . .'

He propped himself up on his elbows and smiled down. 'It doesn't matter a d- tinker's cuss, does it, what people say. You know what you are. *I* know. Lordy, how I know! Oh, Alex, I could . . .'

He had never kissed me with such force, nor, it must be said, I him. I had a sudden vision of Deborah Kerr in her famous beach scene, rolling around in the surf. There must be something about beaches.

'Wow,' I said when I could get a breath. 'What are you grinning at?'

'How could anyone even think it? When you can kiss like that? Oh Alex, sweet maid, will you wait for me while I sit these lousy exams?'

'Will you wait for me while I sit mine? And plough up and down a swimming pool?'

'And while I go to Dartmouth?'

'And while I go to Rome? And get my degree?' It sounds for ever, an awful long time, is it fair to ask anyone to wait that long?

No answers were needed. Some time later we shook the black sand out of our hair, packed up the lunch things, I did up my shirt and we walked back along the beach. Dad wasn't ready to head for town yet, he said, grimly casting his line into the water swirling below the rocks, because he'd promised Gran he wouldn't return without a fish. So we walked slowly on up the headland.

We lay silently for a very long time, just lying in a patch of long grass and looking out to sea, picking out the king waves rolling towards their final magnificent ending against the rocks. Andy's arm was around my shoulders, and we drew warmth from each other as the sun slid towards the horizon, a chill in the air reminding us it was still only August.

What lay ahead for us? I felt like I was leaving something behind on that beach, saying goodbye to something. I don't know, my childhood perhaps, the carefree life? Tomorrow, tonight, we'd be back to the reality of routine, work, swot, train, towards the hardest goals we'd ever set ourselves. Here, on this craggy headland, watching the sun slide towards the sea and the sky change colour, only the sad, magic *now* mattered. We must have slept . . .

'He's caught something.'

Blinked awake, I could see the figure far below us on the slab of rock, the rod bending. 'Dad'll be pleased.'

'Look!' said Andy as the figure staggered backwards

and the rod nearly bent in half. 'He might need help.'

'You go on, Andy. My leg, I don't want to . . . hurrying . . .' And by the time I got down the steep path, the fish had been landed: a handsome enormous snapper. It was thrashing around so much that Dad was having difficulty holding it down for the *coup de grâce*. I couldn't watch. Rock against skull, thud, thud, thud.

'A beaut, Mr Archer,' said Andy. They both looked like grinning kids.

'Ten pounds at least. Baked snapper tomorrow night, squeeze of lemon, enough for everyone. You'll have to come and share it with us, Andy.'

I was more sorry for the fish. Did there always have to be winners and losers? I turned my back on the rocks and the surf and the pale green sky, even on Andy to whom I'd said a sort of temporary good-bye up there on the headland, and began to walk up the road to the beach house. It was time to go home and get on with it.

Did you say stroke faster, Andy? I'll try, oh I'll try, though my lungs are bursting.

Through the splash, through bathing cap tight against ears, I can hear the roar of the crowd. It must be loud.

They don't care who wins, not really. It's just a good race to them, another good battle, like gladiators in the Roman arena slogging it out. One dies, one will live, they don't care which.

But Mr Jack cares, and my family cares like hell, even Jamie in his own funny way, and Andy does, would have, does.

You care, Alex . . . more than anyone, you care, says Andy. So get cracking.

How much does she still have, Andy? Between me and Rome, me and oblivion—between Maggie the winner and me the loser . . .

10

I thought the schedule Mr Jack doled out at five thirty the next morning was a bit rough for the first morning back, convalescent leg and (shush) sort of nervous breakdown (just a little one, nothing too serious) and all. 'One mile straight, half arms only, we'll keep off the kicking . . .' so it went on, up to three miles. He didn't bat an eyelid. Neither did I. Two can play that game. I got in and did it.

The water felt and tasted like salt soup and after about three lengths I knew I was back to the medieval eye torture again. My arms ached, and worse, I seemed to have caught a cold, maybe from the one swim we'd had with Dad out at the beach, which was freezing cold and the surf looked from water level absolutely monstrous. When I finally climbed out of the pool I thought my head was on fire.

Among the few other serious swimmers ploughing up and down I noticed no sign of Maggie, and said so to Mr Jack.

'You've got to know sometime. She's in Aussie for three weeks.'

'Doing what?'

'Training up in Queensland, with some of the Aussie squad.'

'She can't do that.'

'Why not? It's a free world.'

'Because . . . they don't coach Kiwis over there.'
What I meant was, it isn't fair. Maggie hadn't told
me she was going; I could hardly blame her.

'Perhaps no one ever asked before. Maggie's Mum
did, apparently. So there she is.'

Being sharpened up by one of the best coaches in
the world, no doubt at some considerable cost. How
badly Mrs Benton wanted that Olympic blazer for
Maggie; time and money were no object. If it wasn't
for me, she'd waltz in. No wonder Mrs Benton hated
me so.

That explained the morning's heavy schedule. I
knew I was being watched, to see how I could take
it.

I could take it—the programme of sprints and time
trials (arms only, because my leg was aching a bit)
that followed at four thirty, and again twice the next
day, and into next week. The eyes and the sinus
problem didn't get any better, but I'd become used
to that pain.

Two or three hours' swot when the blur cleared
and I could actually see the print in my books, and
an hour's piano practice daily, bed at the same time
as the youngest kids, the holidays ground on.

Andy was incommunicado, head down into his
books, although we caught up by phone every two or
three days. I began to wish someone had told me I
had to give up training for exams. Every time the
sting in my eyes got so bad I thought I really couldn't
bear it, I pictured Mrs Benton sunning herself by the
side of a pool in Queensland, sipping a gin and tonic,

talking earnestly to the Aussie coach, and Maggie keeping up with those Aussie whizz kids in that nice clean pale blue sunny sparkling *cold* water that didn't leave your eyes burning like coals.

Far from the picture of Queensland health, Maggie looked grim when she walked into the pool the first morning back after the holidays. Resting at the end of my first half-mile, I saw her come in alone, say a few words to her coach, but none to anyone else and get straight down to business.

I hoped, being naturally curious, we'd end up in the dressing-room together. I'd just finished my hot shower when she came in.

'Hi Maggie. How was Queensland?'

I thought she might be bashful, or embarrassed, but I was wrong. She looked at me briefly and then started peeling her togs off. Her hip bones were sticking out, and her arms thinner.

'OK.'

'I heard you'd gone. What a tan, lucky you!'

'It won't last long.'

'Hard work? Harder than here?'

'Not really. Just more people, crowded lanes. Each coach had his own special time.'

'Nice clear water, I bet. Your eyes'll have to get used to this soup all over again.'

She didn't reply. I decided I'd tried hard enough to be pleasant. We finished changing in silence. 'See you,' I said casually as I left. Be like that.

If I thought I was the only one with problems, I was wrong again. Gradually, word got about—as it always does—that Maggie had a few, too.

Like having a monumental row with her mother in Australia because she wanted, among other things, to go to a drive-in movie with an Aussie swimmer she'd met, and wasn't allowed. Like her coach here being upset that he wasn't consulted about the Aussie junket. And Mrs Benton coming back loaded with schedules that didn't quite fit in with his ideas, and how he and Mrs Benton had had a row (on the phone the night before Maggie had reappeared at the pool), and she'd threatened to send Maggie to Mr Jack for coaching. And the only reason Maggie was not continuing training in Australia was because she had to live a certain time in New Zealand to qualify for Olympic nomination, and so on. All good clean fun.

Knowing all this, a small bit in the paper during the week was interesting for what it didn't say. 'AUS-TRALIAN EXPERIENCE FOR MAGGIE BENTON' was the headline. 'Olympic swim hopeful Maggie Benton returned this week after three weeks' intense coaching with the famed Australian squad in Queensland.

'Her mother, Mrs Harold Benton, said that Miss Benton had gained invaluable training and time-trial experience alongside swimmers who were expected to make strong bids for the Australian Olympic team next year.

' "They were very impressed with her improvement and her potential. She was offered a place in the squad, which is of course a great honour, but she has her own coach here and her schooling has to be considered."

'Miss Benton has resumed normal twice-daily training. Arch-rival Alex Archer has also started training after suffering a hockey injury to her leg in June, which kept her out of the water for six weeks. They are expected to have their first clash at an invitation meeting on 24 November.'

'Would've been interesting', Mr Jack said the morning this appeared and he told me about Mrs Benton threatening to send Maggie to him for coaching. 'Both of you together.'

By what divine right did Mrs Benton assume that he'd automatically take her darling Maggie for coaching?

'No thanks,' I said. 'If that happens, I'm retiring. It's me or her.'

I was not joking. The winter seemed never-ending. Swot was never-ending. Early training, the same three miles day after day, seemed pointless. My leg still ached. Eyes were permanently red-rimmed and sinuses permanently stuffy. Calisthenics, without Andy to do exercises with, was a bore. Weights got heavier. Piano lessons, with little practice to speak of, were a sham. School was dreary, my family too noisy, Gran too busy with her baby dresses and Andy so deep into his books he'd disappeared from sight.

I really had begun to wonder if it was worth it, when Maggie plainly had it sewn up. Why didn't I just gently fade out, not enter for meetings, forget about Rome. Or 'announce my retirement'—one story, one photo, promptly forgotten. Alex, the might-have-been if only she'd stuck at it.

At least Maggie and I were talking again. It turned out that she'd hated Aussie. The coach had talked down his nose about our little Kiwi cousin and got rather upset when she'd beaten one of his bright hopes in a time trial. Whereupon her mother had got in on the act and talked about paying him good money ('Alex, I could have died, right on the side of the pool they were') and she was known thereafter as the Kiwi dragon-lady. The swimmers themselves were OK, but the only one who really understood was the boy she'd not been allowed to go out with. She was still writing to him and if all went well they'd both be in their Olympic teams next year—'Ooops,' said Maggie. 'That wasn't very tactful, was it?' 'That's OK,' I said.

Maggie told me all this, because we understand each other, even though her mother and reporters and everyone else seem to think that because we both want the same thing and only one of us can have it, we can't be civilized to each other. Let's face it, when you train in the same pool, use the same dressing-room, line up for the same races together as long as we have, you'd have to have a lot of stamina to be anything but civilized.

She still has something, Alex. You'll have to try harder.

I can't.

I think you can.

It's not fair, for a trip to hang on the result of one race!

Consider yourself luckier than the Americans. They have trials for their Olympic teams. It doesn't matter if you hold a world record, if you get beaten in the trials, that's it. One trial, one race, one chance.

Perhaps they might send both of us?

It's possible. Your times are good enough.

Even if she wins this, I hold the national record.

You're on your way to another.

You're kidding.

Honest. First lap was under thirty seconds. Turn wasn't too hot, you lost about point four there . . .

And lost the race.

Oh no. She's only got about six inches on you now.

That's all? No kidding?

That's all. Dig in, girl . . .

11

At school, as the third term swung into action, I kept a low profile. There were a few remarks in the first assembly about the great success of the production, with some outstanding work by soloists, etcetera. People round me looked sideways, sniggered, nudged each other; I looked blankly at my shoes and ignored them.

Auditions were being held for a revue to be put on during the last week of term after exams. To my own surprise I was tempted. It was to be extracts from musicals: *South Pacific*, *Oklahoma!*, *My Fair Lady*, *West Side Story*, even something called *The Sound of Music* which had lots of kids in it and was in rehearsal and due to open on Broadway in November. A friend who had something to do with stage management had written to tell Miss Macrae the music was superb, he was sending some of the songs, including a delightful number called 'Doh-Ray-Mi'.

I thought of Andy and how I'd love to sing a Coward song, as a sort of gift. Miss Macrae bailed me up; how would I like to do just one solo, and perhaps a trio? There'd only be a few rehearsals in the last two weeks when exams were over and everyone was just having fun and packing up for the holidays. I agreed.

Our end-of-second-term exam marks came back. Moderate in most, brilliant in none, and History, where I'd usually been one of the top two, a disaster. Not even a pass, forty-one in fact, about thirteenth out of twenty. When the mark was read out, with rather undue emphasis, it felt like an actual blow. I put my head down on the desk, and looked at no one. When it was time for break I walked outside to the farthest corner of the playing-fields.

Julia caught me up, put her hand on my shoulder. 'Don't.'

'Alex, it's only a silly test, a practice run.'

I strode on, towards blurred trees. 'Go away, Julia.'

'Wasn't that the exam you fell asleep in? No wonder. You probably did half of it quite well. Forget it, Alex.'

How could I? The shame! I'd lost the security of knowing that even without much effort I could end up somewhere near the top. Worse, perhaps even really trying, I might not get the School Certificate marks I wanted . . . That would be a bitter pill. I'd *always* been in the first three.

We'd reached the boundary trees. I slumped down on to one of the surface roots. 'Leave me alone.'

'Your other marks weren't so bad . . .'

'Five weeks to School C . . .'

'For heaven's sake,' said Julia. 'What does getting School C mean to you? Nothing.'

'Of course it means . . .'

'Just one easy tiny step up the ladder towards fame and fortune. You don't expect to fail, now, do you?' Her voice was rich with scorn. 'I'm sick of you, Alex

Archer, moping around the place, grizzling about training and swot and all the other things you choose to do. Some people actually have to *work* just to pass. Some people work and still don't pass.'

'I am not some people.'

'Oh no, we're special we are. Look, Alex, you've got everything going for you. You can do anything you want, you're good at every single thing you try, your parents worship the ground you tread on . . .'

'They don't.'

'Oh yes, they do. If you decided you were going to be the first woman Prime Minister or fly to the moon they'd say fine, Alex, how can we help.'

'All right, I'm lucky . . .'

'Don't you notice anything? I rang you last night, with some great news, but you came rushing into class late, forgetting me completely . . .'

She had rung too, sounding most peculiar, promising to tell all before school.

'. . . expecting everyone to excuse you because *you've* been *training*, and forty-one for History is of course far more important. Oh, the shame, not to be in the top few . . .'

She'd put her finger right on it, perceptive Julia.

'What the hell does it matter?' she went on. 'How would you like to be sitting School Certificate knowing that your whole future depended on it? My whole future, being a doctor—three hundred marks, and a scholarship, that's the deal with Dad . . .'

'What are you talking about? What deal?'

She was flushed, breathing noisily, trying to get the air in and out of her lungs, and I knew an attack was coming. It all came out then, about this second cousin from Australia, who'd seemed so nice, so interested in her career. About him coming to the house one Saturday when she was alone, and her feeling very uncomfortable. Nothing specific, just . . . Anyway, there'd been several occasions and then he went skiing too, with the family, and he kept getting on the tow bars with her and putting a protective arm around her, and then yesterday, he'd been there again, after school. Mum was out shopping in the car, and he tried to kiss her and had actually started undoing his fly, but he didn't choose his moment very well . . . 'Dad came out of his study, we didn't know he'd come home early from work. I rushed off to my room, and I heard a bit of a row between them, but then they both came in, Cousin Mario full of apologies, didn't know what came over him, would never happen again, and my dear father playing it down. Mario was just feeling affectionate, and he *was* half-Italian as if somehow that excused him, and I mustn't tell Mum because it would upset her, she was very fond of Mario. Well, after I stopped crying I'd had a bit of time to think, and I thought what would you have done, all I could think of was you might have given him the old knees up or socked him in the jaw because you're a whole lot bigger and stronger than me . . . Anyway, Dad seemed so concerned not to upset Mario or Mum, never mind about me, that I suddenly thought, I'll keep quiet in return for being allowed to apply for medical school.'

'You didn't!'

'I did. Dad was furious but Mario, all smarm and

cringe, persuaded him that I should be allowed to try. To save a bit of face he had to say three hundred for School C, *and* a scholarship . . .'

'That's steep.'

'But it gives me something to aim at. I don't think either of them believe I'll make it. But I will.'

My quiet friend Julia, who would have believed it? She looked so pleased with herself I had to give her a hug.

'So that's all. Dad would kill me if he knew I'd told you. He was still pretty angry at breakfast this morning. He was even angrier when I produced a piece of paper with all this written down and asked him to sign it, in front of Mum so that he couldn't protest.'

'You did? Oh boy.'

She shrugged as I chortled. 'Mario's going back to Australia. The funny thing is, I felt dirty, ashamed; as if it was somehow my fault. How was I so brave, Alex?'

She shook one of her little yellow pills into her hand, and popped it under her tongue. I gave her a back rub until it took effect, and until her heart had stopped racing.

'How? Does it matter? You did it. I'm so proud of you—and sorry for being such a pain.' If people saw us together under the trees and wanted to think strange and weird thoughts, well, it's all in the mind, as the Goons keep telling us.

I remember reading some actress saying that a woman's greatest pleasure is taking her corsets off at night. I wouldn't know because I've never worn corsets, but it's fairly obvious she hasn't sat exams, because there's nothing like the feeling of joy and relief you get as you hand in your last exam paper.

My last one was Music, with six others. Even as we agreed it was the last exam we'd ever sit—there was only University Entrance next year and all of us expected to be accredited—I knew I personally was talking nonsense. If I was going to do law there'd be four or five years of exams, tests, essays.

Today, however, I am free, free, *free*. Julia still has two to go, and she's so grimly determined to get her three hundred marks she's working like it's going out of fashion. I've arranged to meet Andy at the Olympic Pool because he had his last scholarship exam today and we are going to celebrate in the sparkling clean blue champagne water. I am floating with freedom—no hockey, no swot until one in the morning, no ballet, no piano (I did that exam two weeks ago and strangely was quite pleased with a modest Pass Plus), no teachers reading out forty-one for History, no school shows except for the little revue, not even any school because we have two weeks off as a reward before the last two weeks which are a fun time anyway. Then it's the long holidays and Christmas and the run-up to the nationals where I am going to do brilliantly and beat Maggie and get nominated for Rome.

That's what I thought. I'd sorted myself out, stopped trying to do so much, staggered through what Dad has called 'a difficult year'. Now I had only to train, with the gorgeous Andy alongside, up and down the lengths that make up my daily three miles. And when training is finished we can lie in the sun and talk to our hearts' content, and if there is no one too near we might kiss and he'll serenade me with Noel Coward.

Or so I thought.

Mr Jack and Dad had planned my programme and my races carefully between now and the nationals. An invitation club meeting in three weeks, on 24 November. Another, three weeks later. Then a long gap over Christmas/New Year when I'd put in some really hard slog. Taper off a little for the Auckland champs which start on 15 January. Four events in that. Then the final run-up to the nationals in Napier starting 10 February. As usual, I'd be missing the second week of school.

Normally, Mr Jack would have wanted more races than this to sharpen me up, but he'd decided that I'd only meet Maggie at the big events, which would no doubt be of some interest to the papers. Therefore I'd be sharpening up with lots of time trials against Andy and the boys of the squad; no inter-club meetings or long bus trips out of town.

My first appearance/performance was not a success. Nothing actually went wrong. I didn't fall off the starting-block, or jump the gun, or muff my turn. I didn't foul the rope or hit my head on the end of the pool, or swallow a mouthful or get cramp. I didn't get the evil eye from Mrs Benton. It wasn't pouring with rain, or freezing cold or blowing a gale up the pool. I didn't have to wait until ten thirty at night. I did have my favourite togs on.

Maggie just started off better than last season, that's all, while I started off worse. I did sixty-eight point one seconds, two seconds down on my best one hundred and ten yards, that's a lot. While she, sharpened up by her Aussie experience, did a sixty-six seconds, point two faster than her best last season, a record.

I felt like I was swimming through glue. Towards the end I felt the first stabs of cramp in my left calf. I was still carrying a few pounds of extra weight. I was only half-way fit . . . I felt stale. Already.

'For a first outing . . .' said Mr Jack, staring at his stop-watch.

'Not good. Lousy in fact. Alex could do better. In ten weeks' time, will she pull through? Will she make it? Will she achieve her heart's desire? Listen to the next thrilling episode . . .'

'Pipe down, Alex,' said Andy, sitting next to Mr Jack, looking equally grim. Dad on the other side completed a dismal trio, the Marx brothers at a funeral. 'You talk too much at times.'

Of course I do, because I can't bear the sound of my own silence. It howls failure at me, and asks me why I bother, when Maggie will be a perfectly splendid rep for her country, very trim in her black blazer. It reminds me of everything my family has done to get me this far, not forgetting Gran who works her fingers to the bone and helps Mum the way I should help her if I were ever at home, nor the brats whom I hardly see and who don't see as much of Dad as they might because he's always driving me to training or someplace else . . .

Not even Andy gripping my hand tightly helped to soothe my awful premonition that things were not going to improve.

Nothing is simple, everything gets complicated, and even the following day got out of control. 'Come sailing,' Andy said, as we were leaving the pool after the race. 'You need a blow-out. You're getting too earnest. Again.'

'Don't you start.'

It wasn't a day I would have chosen for my introduction to small boats, to find out what made Andy, the future sailor, tick. I held things while Andy rigged the yacht, with what he described as a twenty-knot westerly rattling the sail in anticipation. Only the male of the species, and mad ones at that, seemed to be out on the harbour today.

'Get in,' he yelled. 'Port side, hang on to the jibsheet.'

'What side? The what?'

'That rope there.'

It was all go: movement, wind, waves, spray, rocking, noise, tangles, shouts, total confusion. Andy was pushing, leaping, climbing in, leaning over the stern, pulling ropes, the boat already taking off. I was, as they say, totally at sea.

'Stack out,' he yelled, and when I looked blank, 'Lean out, balance. That's better. Yippeeeeee.'

I could even laugh with exhilaration, and not a little fright. We were screaming away from the beach, leaning over, plunging into the waves so that within seconds my shorts were soaked. Of Andy the sailor, grinning, balancing tiller, ropes, stacking out so that he seemed to be attached to the boat only by his toenails, seemingly in superb control, I was in complete awe.

I thought, even as yet another wave came up to drench my backside, I could get quite keen on this.

'Where're we going?' I yelled.

'You choose.'

'I don't mind. How do you change direction?'

If we'd stuck to the sailing lesson, it would have been a wonderful day. We tried tacking, reaching, running, even my first hair-raising gybe, and then set sail for North Head and around the corner, Cheltenham Beach for lunch. We lay in the sun to dry out a bit, and then walked up North Head. The seascape glittered, silver and turquoise, at our feet. Dozens of the big keelers were heading for the city, returning from the islands of the gulf. The city volcanoes lay round and green in the haze. 'Kipling said it all, didn't he, in six words,' said Andy. 'There's not a harbour like it.'

Being so busy sailing, I'd been able to forget last night's terrible race, until, for reasons best known to himself, Andy chose to remind me on the return journey, when we were reaching comfortably back towards Orakei.

'I felt for you, last night. You looked so sluggish, not like you at all.'

'Not now, Andy.'

'I hate to see you . . .'

'Lose? I've done that plenty of times, even if only to Maggie.'

'No, I mean, working so hard, flogging yourself, for what? You're investing an awful lot of time . . .'

'Wouldn't you, if you had the chance of a trip to Rome? What are you trying to say? Are you ever so gently advising me to get out, now? Don't you think I'm going to make it?'

'It's not that.'

'Then what is it?' Oh, he'd touched a nerve. 'Did you bring me sailing just to show me what I'm missing, and hint that I'm wasting my time doing four miles a day because it's as clear as the nose on your face . . .'

'Alex, calm down.'

I didn't even stop to see how far we were from a beach.

'I will not be told to calm down. And if that's the way you feel . . . I can do a bit more training, right here and now.'

Somehow I got out of the boat, fell, dived, I don't know. Andy's horrified face flashed by. The water felt warm. I came up spluttering, saw the beach, trees, houses that looked as near as any others, and began swimming. In shorts and sweater, with the chop of the waves, it wasn't easy. I knew even I would begin to tire pretty quickly.

'Alex!' I heard shouts, the rattle of the boat nearby. Andy must have turned quickly. '*Alex.*'

I stopped swimming and began to tread water. Some people did harbour races for fun. Was it the season for sharks?

'Alex, get in.'

'No.'

'Get *in*.'

'I'm training.'

'You're just being bloody-minded, pulling a stunt. Now get in. You can't swim that far . . . It's over a mile . . .'

'Rubbish,' I spluttered, though I suspected he was right. I was tiring just with the effort of keeping my head and clothed body above the chop. I started to take my sweater off, but even that meant treading water very fast. 'I swim . . . twice as far . . . every morning.'

'Not out here, you don't.'

Being bloody-minded, and angry, I swam over to the boat, threw in my sweater and set off again, now in shirt and shorts. The water didn't look that bad.

'*Alex*.' There was real anger in his voice. I must have swum for fifty yards, no more, when I heard his voice again, closer. I stopped and looked up.

He was furious, afraid, all at once. 'You can't run away for ever. *Get in*.'

'I'm not . . .' but I'd caught a mouthful, and when he held out the paddle, I hung on to it with some relief.

'You can't run away, you can't always be in control, and you can't always get what you want . . . OK, be pig-headed, get swimming, if you don't make it, for the rest of my life I'll be the guy who took his girl-friend sailing and d-drowned her.'

I coughed and spluttered.

He yelled, 'Just because I said something you didn't want to hear. Can you do *that*, Alex?'

I knew I couldn't. And the tide was carrying us

out, away from the waterfront. Against chop, wind and tide I had no show. I let go the paddle and swam to the boat.

'Get in over the stern.' Somehow, pulling, kicking, hauling, dragging myself and being dragged, I got back on board. In the wind I was instantly cold, and there was a long red gouge down my thigh where I'd dragged over a screw or something sharp.

'There's a parka up front. Wet, but it'll keep the wind off. Put it on.'

But I could only sit, shaking, rocking, as the boom flogged to and fro. We looked at each other, and had the same thought, for in the bottom of that madly rocking boat, two very wet and tired people had a long and grateful cuddle.

'We do choose some funny places,' I said. 'You *know* why I'm trying for Rome. Why do you have to cross-examine me, as if I'm in court? Why does anyone do anything?'

'They climb Everest because it's there. What did Ed Hillary say, "We knocked the bastard off." '

'Rome's my Everest then. I can't give up now. After six seasons . . .'

'I know, but it's hard for the people around you . . .'

'That's no reason . . .'

'Allow me some concern, Alex. You're so damn stubborn, sometimes you're right, but not always. You were right about Helensville. You were wrong just now. The sea doesn't respect anger or any sort of arrogance. The sea will always win.'

I could see how far the tide had taken us. I wouldn't

have got home against that. 'OLYMPIC SWIM PROSPECT DROWNS IN HARBOUR' . . .

He gave me the bailing tin, and began pulling in ropes to get the boat sailing before we both froze to death. The brilliant sunshine was no match for the wind across my goose pimples. We gybed back on course and sat close together on the long beat home, thigh to thigh. I decided I liked Andy the Masterful, taking charge.

I've been thinking what you said about both of us going to Rome, Andy. I read something this week, that swimming commentator in the Weekly News, some old boy who's been doing it for years. Anyway, predictions:

'Whatever the outcome of the national titles, serious consideration should be given to sending both these talented girls to Rome. Their intense rivalry over five seasons has already inspired a new generation of juniors and can only go on benefitting the sport.

'Miss Benton has the more impressive score of titles and records over the seasons, and has proved herself a consistent and graceful champion. But time and time again she has been pushed to these achievements by the brave and determined Miss Archer, whose potential is, if anything, the greater. One must win the lion's share in Napier, but both should be considered worthy for Rome . . .' Isn't that great?

Alex, you're d-dodging the issue, already looking for boltholes . . .

I am not . . .

Yes you are. Don't you realize you're absolutely neck-and-neck. Twenty yards to go and you're already justifying second place . . . hoping it will be good enough for Rome.

All right then, I am. I simply cannot go any faster. And I've got my period, a week early. My body is telling me something.

So? It has never worried you in the past. You've won races with your period before.

You know me too well.

Wasn't this win for me?

Perhaps I just haven't got what it takes, not really. I should've listened to you that day when I jumped off your boat, saved myself a whole lot of work. You were right.

I was wrong. But you've got to do it. No one can win for you. Oh, keep trying, sweet maid . . . Hold on . . .

12

The last two weeks of school were always fun, and did I need it, some light relief to counteract training morning and night, as heavy as it had ever been, weights and calisthenics daily. Over the other side of the pool, Maggie ploughed up and down solo, did her time trials against the stop-watch and her mother's constant presence.

Only knowing that Andy would be there, diving in with me, alongside in the water for length after length, made it bearable. I had to work hard to keep up with him. Looking back, those few weeks in November, despite that awful first race, I was never happier, freer. I had a birthday, with Andy included in a family party. His present was a single pearl on a gold chain.

At school we had no lessons to speak of, instead, class discussion, films, trips to the art gallery, packing up books, extra swimming and tennis time, rehearsals for the revue, almost holidays already.

On the last day of term, at prize-giving, we'd find out the prefects for next year. Drawing up our own lists, it seemed everyone thought I was a dead cert. A wee voice inside said perhaps they'd do the dirty on this dead cert like they did with the hockey team;

my turn in 1961, in the Upper Sixth, when I'd been, or not been, to Rome.

First rehearsal for the revue was posted for lunchtime the first day back. One perfomance only, an hour long, Miss Macrae told her singers in the Music Room. The sixth formers who'd been accredited had been working on some skits and funny songs. 'Alex, Janice,' she called, 'what about a couple of numbers from *Oklahoma!*, "Oh What a Beautiful Morning", "Surrey with the Fringe on Top" or "I'm Just a Girl Who Can't Say No". Who'd like to have a go at that? Alex?'

Beside me, Julia snorted. I did not appreciate the unsubtle dig. That Alex was light years ago. (If she is, said my wee voice, what are you doing here? Shut up, I can have a bit of fun, I told the voice firmly. It's all in school time, Mum and Dad need never know.)

'You talked about a Noel Coward song. I'd rather do one of those,' I said.

'Very well. Janice, you can do *Oklahoma!*, have a look through the score here. You saw the film, didn't you? Alex, what about "Mad Dogs and Englishmen"? Or "Don't Put Your Daughter on the Stage, Mrs Worthington"?' She flipped through the book of Coward songs.

One thing, as it always does, led to another. Before I knew where I was, it had been decided thus: an upper sixth former, with a Clara Butt foghorn, would do 'Mad Dogs and Englishmen' dressed in a solar topee and plus fours. Another who was learning to sing properly with beautiful vowels like Julie Andrews would sing 'I'll See You Again' in a long slinky dress. Then I'd come on for the Worthington song dressed à la 1930s, in a check suit and bow tie, with my hair Brylcreemed back. 'You'll make a handsome young man, more so now you're taller,' said Miss Macrae, who'd known me since Third Form. Alarm bells went off. They continued jangling while the group threw around some more ideas.

'Can't I do one of those Gertrude Lawrence numbers, romantic, in a dress?' I asked plaintively. Miss Macrae didn't even hear me. Then some sixth former I wish I'd killed on the spot said, 'Why doesn't Alex do her song dressed as you, Miss Macrae, she'd bring the house down, you're always saying the stage is no career for anyone with any sense. In one of your suits and her hair grey and a cushion down her front . . .' She stopped, face scarlet, hand to mouth and we were all relieved when Fish-face threw back her head and roared with laughter. It was decided.

And why, you are asking, did I put my head in the noose once again. Various reasons. One, my time trials were so dreadful I really did need something to make me laugh. Two, I wanted to make an audience laugh again. Three, I dreaded even trying, but surely this was foolproof, taking off a teacher most people thought was a bit of a joke. Four, I can't resist a challenge. I'm a show-off, all right then, a great show-off, but aren't all performers, and showing off is also an urge to share, and what is so wrong with that? I intended to do the song well, even dressed as Miss Macrae with a cushion down my front and feeling a great ninny.

The song was a long one and took me a couple of

nights to learn, *sotto voce* so that no one could hear noises coming from my bedroom. I had two practices with Miss Codlin in the music room. The words were fun to sing. No wonder Andy was a fan of Coward.

She's a bit of an ugly duckling
You must honestly confess,
And the width of her seat
Would surely defeat
Her chances of success . . .
On my knees Mrs Worthington,
Please, Mrs Worthington,
Don't put your daughter on the stage.

How I put it across would be left to me, said Miss Macrae. I could work it out with some of the others. 'Watch the way I walk. How do I sit in a chair, legs crossed, apart? I use my hands a lot, gestures? My large voice, how will you get the impression of that across in a song? We'll have to let down the hem of one of my more repellent suits. Make-up won't be hard, a few lines here and there. Hair greyed, would you mind cutting the fringe a little shorter? A cushion, as Jane so rightly said, down your front. Well, this will be a new experience for me, too.'

Which brings me, reluctantly, dreadfully, to the morning of 2 December, a date which is for ever carved into my heart. Sunday morning, early training as usual. I cycled out of the house, sun already up, a bonus after all those gloomy pre-dawn sessions through the winter and spring. Andy was not at the pool, but then he didn't come to every single session, and he had some sort of school function last night to which, as a prefect, he was obliged to go. Three miles, time trials marginally better, although I could tell Maggie's over the other side of the pool were better again.

No plans for the rest of the day, apart from training again at four and a loose arrangement with Andy to take a picnic lunch somewhere. We might drive over the bridge and have lunch on North Head again, watching the yachts, and then go for a swim.

I knew from the minute I walked in the back door something was odd. No kid's breakfast session blaring *The Story of the Little Red Engine* or Danny Kaye singing 'Tubby the Tuba' through the house. No kids, not even out playing in the garden on this lovely summer morning.

Gran in the kitchen, clearing up breakfast, but no welcome to speak of. Just a little bent back at the sink washing dishes, saying: 'Your Mum wants to see you in your bedroom, Alex,' in response to my 'Where's everyone?' She sounded a bit sniffly. I hoped she wasn't getting a cold, because sometimes they went to her chest.

What had I done? Had Mum found out about the Macrae thing at school? Surely it wasn't that serious, just a bit of fun . . .

Mum was sitting on my unmade bed. Something was up, I could see that. 'Sit down, Alex. Shut the door.'

'OK,' I said lightly. 'What's up doc?'

One thing about Mum, she comes straight to the point.

'I had a ring from Mr Richmond this morning. Andy was knocked off his bike around eleven o'clock last night, riding home from a school function. A drunken driver in an E-type Jag, leaving a party, no lights on, came tearing out of a driveway at fifty miles an hour. He didn't have a chance. He died on the way to hospital.'

'No.'

'I'm sorry, Alex . . .'

'No. Not Andy, never. He heard the car coming and stopped just in time . . . He's in hospital, broken legs, the car only ran over his legs. Soon fixed . . .'

Mum had moved over and was kneeling at my feet, looking up at me. 'Alex, he died on the way to hospital. There was nothing that could be done. The driver of the Jag didn't even stop . . .'

I stared down at her. All I could see was her brown wet wise eyes, waiting for me to crack. The rest was darkness, ringing noises in my ears, the crash of chrome on metal, crunch of tyres running over bones, blood, blood and more blood . . .

'No!'

'Alex, my baby . . . Come here . . .'

I slid down off the chair into her arms. Gran told me later I screamed. Well, so what. I can remember folding myself into the smallest ball possible and burying myself in Mum's enclosing arms. We sat there, on the floor, for hours, rocking, drowning in my tears.

You can only cry for so long. When every tear had been wrung, I'd filled several of Dad's large hankies that she thoughtfully produced. Wise Mum. And when you can't bear the grief, you make arrangements.

191

'Can you run me over to see his parents?'

'Now?'

'Yes.'

I don't remember much of that visit, except certain very vivid details. His mother was in a state of shock, just sitting in a chair. Mr Richmond shook me silently by the hand. I was about to embrace him, but the phone rang. Three calls later, with me sitting beside Mrs Richmond and getting absolutely no response from whatever I said, not even from taking her limp hand and holding it tightly, it was clear the best thing I could do was go home. I didn't wait for him to come off the phone. Some impulse took me along the corridor and along to the bedroom, Andy's Room with a View. I opened the door and stood for a while waiting for my eyes to get accustomed to the shadows. It was like I was taking a photograph, capturing every detail. This was one room I'd not been in. Going along with his father's idea of what was proper, we'd always gone to the study when we wanted to talk.

The bed had not been slept in. Stuff lay everywhere as in my room. A large transistor radio, yesterday's towel on the floor. Balsa wood aeroplanes, made when he was a child, hanging from the ceiling; even more models of ships and pictures of ships, warships and sailing ships. Hadn't his parents realized? Text books on physics, marine engineering, maths, war stories, sea books and ship books, Lawrence Durrell, Kingsley Amis, Robert Graves' *Greek Myths*, books everywhere. Behind the closed curtains lay the famous View across the harbour. 'Last, loneliest . . .' How terribly true.

I looked again at the bed, made but crumpled with the imprint of someone who'd put his feet up for a while. Right next to the alarm clock, in a modest frame, was a photo of me. I put it in my shirt pocket.

Mr Richmond was still on the phone, so I walked quietly past, gesturing goodbye. He put his hand over the receiver. 'Just a moment, sorry, Alex . . . toll calls. Do you have to go? Thank you . . .' and had to blow his nose before he could continue. I kissed him on the cheek and felt the tremor under his skin.

Returning home to a subdued Sunday lunch, with the family being abnormally polite to each other, training again that afternoon—I'd turned to ice. The strange thing was that people didn't say *anything*, most people anyway. Everyone knew we'd been going steady for the best part of six months. Apart from Mr Jack, who looked almost as dreadful as I felt, and Julia, and a few others, most people avoided me, their eyes looked away. It was almost as though it had never happened, Andy had never existed. Even Maggie was speechless. She mumbled a few words at the end of training. She was, I realized, embarrassed.

It was the same at school. Groups of two or three talking, suddenly silent. Andy had been well known, like you'd expect when he was six foot two and played in the First Fifteen. Julia shielded me with the knack of knowing when a touch of her arm would help.

I suppose it got around the staff room. We suspected the staff knew a good deal about our out-of-school doings, especially different pupils like me.

Miss Gillies called me into her study and talked directly about the tragedy of young death. 'People will tell you you'll forget. They're wrong. Even if this young man had not turned out to be your future partner, you won't forget.' She said it with such conviction I believed she had been through it herself. There'd been two wars, so it was pretty likely. Who would ever know?

Miss Macrae didn't mince words, either. She made me talk about him, about the dreadful unfairness of being in the wrong place at the wrong split second of time, why him, why, *why*? 'Life is not fair, Alex. You are just learning a little earlier than most, and harder.' But I felt better after the tears. 'You won't, of course, be doing Mrs Worthington. It was a good idea. Maybe next year. I'll still be around.'

But I won't, I thought. I'm going to Rome. For him. I'm going to Rome.

I sat with Mum and Dad at the back of the church for the funeral, staring at the dark wooden walls and the rows of relatives and business friends in black suits, a large contingent from his school in their navy school shorts, lots of men who were obviously teachers. Some uncle also with a stutter (a family thing?) gave a dreary speech, gloomily recounting Andy's achievements in 'his tragically short life'. I just wept, I couldn't stop and I couldn't care who saw me. When the very long coffin went by at the end, carried by Mr Richmond and a lot of elderly men, I thought I was going to explode with anguish.

'Rest in Peace,' the man said. How could he, when

he hadn't said goodbye and every cell in his body must have been screaming 'This is it' the split second before the Jaguar hit him and turned him in another split second from a beautiful young man with the body of a Greek god into a bloody corpse.

He would have known, in that last point five of a second. I know how long point five of a second is, the difference between winning and losing, living and dying. If only . . . It makes no sense. Did I save you, Andy, from certain accident at Helensville, only for this? Good choices, bad choices, dark fate, confusion, muddle, all a jumble. And now they carry you past me . . .

Somehow I made it to the car, running from the church via a side door before the hoards of dark suits came down the aisle. I sure wasn't going to go to the crematorium, nor stand around talking and laughing outside the porch, as I'd seen people do at funerals, and even less go to the house to watch his mother, and drink tea and eat cream cakes and make polite conversation. Mum and Dad followed. Mum said I blacked out in the car. I don't remember. I didn't go back to school that day. I went to the pool and swam and swam and swam, maybe something over seven miles, until I was exhausted.

In the sleepless nights that followed I turned from being a sweet maid into an ice maiden, not a very nice person at all. I hung for endless hours in that state half-way between sleep and wakefulness, with a blue Morris Minor and an E-type Jaguar coming straight at me, missing me but leaving me standing on a stage strewn with corpses, like the last act of *Hamlet*. Reading didn't help because the same image kept getting between me and the page. The radio finished at midnight. I took to making myself cups of hot chocolate at three and walking round the garden. I did calisthenics for half an hour, working up such a sweat that I needed to take a shower before getting back into bed. One night I even ended up in Mum's bed, terrified out of my skin, appalled at the thought of another two hours' nightmares before dawn broke and I could reasonably go training.

There were, I decided, two things I could do for Andy. The first was rather weird. I had no idea where it came from or if I had the courage to see it through.

The second was more straightforward. For Andy I'd train harder than I ever trained in my life. Every time trial would be an ordeal, maximum effort, every length a test. For Andy I would beat Maggie at the nationals. Being realistic, it would be part of the plan that she'd probably win the Auckland titles first, though I'd give her a run for her money. But the nationals would be all or nothing. And when I heard my name among the Olympic nominations later in February, it would be my silent private memorial, my gift.

The other thing I was going to do for Andy would be short and sharp, all over and done with next week, three days before the end of school. I found Miss Macrae and asked if it was too late for me to do a song in the Coward bracket for the revue.

'Changed your mind, Alex?' she said, looking at me curiously.

'Not the Worthington thing. Could I do perhaps one of the quieter songs, a duet, like "Room with a View".'

My voice was as nonchalant as I could make it, but my heart was pounding.

'I don't see why not. Let's see, Lorna is doing "I'll See You Again". That would fit in well, you as the young man as we suggested earlier.'

'OK,' I said. She looked puzzled, but said nothing more.

Only Julia knew why. I had to tell her, tell someone, to keep myself sane.

'Alex, you're mad,' she said. 'What if you break down? You look so awful, all that training and no sleep. You've lost weight. Look at the bags under your eyes. I tell you, you'll never get through it.'

'Yes, I will. They didn't make me laugh before, remember . . .'

Julia shook her head, wearily. Looking after me was tiring. She'd lost weight herself after working herself into the ground for her exams. What Julia didn't know was that I was in a strange way looking forward to seeing myself as a young man, if only for an hour. Some sort of tribute? Defiance in the face of those rumours? But as Mum had said, among much else these past few days, we all have our own ways of dealing with grief. Many people get to forty, even older and never have it touch them closely, never see a body or weep until they can weep no more. Some go to church, others escape to their office to work, or rush around doing housework, smiling merrily, fooling everybody except the voice inside that talks to them at night. If mine was to get up and sing his favourite song, so be it.

And the fact that this time I'd *chosen* to wind up playing a male, so that catty little girls and their mothers might again whisper Alex Archer has too many male hormones—that no longer mattered. Andy's gift to me was his breath on my lips, his rough chin on my breasts, telling me (as if I ever really doubted it) that I was everything female. I mightn't be very feminine, but boy, was I female.

People could think what they pleased. If that was something else you had to learn, growing up, again so be it.

I learnt the song in a night, remembering snatches of it from earlier days.

A room with a view—and you,
With no one to worry us,
No one to hurry us—through
This dream we've found,
We'll gaze at the sky—and try
To guess what it's all about
Then we will figure out—why
The world is round.

Simple enough, but also deep enough for me at this time.

. . . and sorrow will never come,
Oh, will it ever come—true,
Our room with a view.

Rehearsals were fitted in among all the other things going on in the last week of school. Miss Macrae seemed quite happy with my small contribution. Dress rehearsal was pretty patchy. We all hoped the skits would go better on the day. Janice, in red gingham with a very low bodice, made a good job of Ado Annie's song, 'I'm Just a Girl', and Clara Butt's 'Mad Dogs' wasn't too bad, either, though I think I'd have done it better. I didn't have a costume yet—a double-breasted suit was being provided by someone's elder brother, about the same height as me.

I was to sing the song downstage right, with Julie Andrews in a soft twilight lighting effect. I wanted something romantic. The school would think it wet, corny even.

Performance was timed for one forty-five. We had a final rehearsal that morning. I could feel the atmosphere getting super-charged, as it did that final *Wizard* night. Me, I was cold as stone.

I put on the shirt and the tie and the suit, which fitted remarkably well. Anyway, I didn't have to move much, just lean against the window frame, and sing. It would all be over in two minutes.

Miss Macrae was directing make-up again, though being only fifth formers upwards most of the girls were doing their own, heavy-handed because when else do they get the chance to plaster it on and mothers not complain? I'd already slicked my hair right back with Brylcreem when I presented my face to her. 'Foundation as usual, then come back.' I did that. My face was set hard as a statue. Julia appeared in the mirror, checking me. I gave her a cold male smile, if there is such a thing, and ignored her. Miss Macrae sat me down in the chair. 'Let's see, won't need much, not with your bone structure, those cheekbones, like Katherine Hepburn. Slightly heavier eyebrows, no lips. Little shading here, and here. Sideburns, no, not in 1930, but just a suggestion of male hair here. Moustache?'

'No.'

'I told you you'd make a handsome young man,' she said, as I stood up. 'Alex, are you all right? You're very quiet.'

'I'm fine.'

A tall young man stared back at me from the full-length mirror. Pale, interesting, quite elegant actually, like something from an old movie. What had she said about cheekbones? I'd never really noticed.

And the suit did fit well. I'd always felt comfortable, even felt a sense of freedom, in the male gear I'd worn for shows over the years. Well, I thought, I don't see why men should have the monopoly on freedom, why girls should have to totter around in tight skirts and stilettoes, from now on I'm wearing slacks, jeans, shoes I can run in if I want or need to.

'Not bad,' said Julia's voice. 'I could fall for you. You've got a nerve, Alex. I just hope . . .'

'Sssh,' I said. To everyone else in the room I was

just Alex doing a song, one of many. Nothing special. It would be counted as rather a boring number.

'Break a leg,' she said. Not a particularly apt remark, all things considered, I thought, as I trooped along the corridor to the school hall with the others.

By the time my turn came I was sweating through the greasepaint. I debated with myself whether I should throw a faint. The school would never miss my number in a thousand years. There was no programme. They'd never know.

Your choice, Alex. Live with it. Which is more choice than Andy had, in that point five of a second. No choice at all. The choice was made by that drunken slob. Andy, innocently riding past on his bike, lost on the first and the last throw of the dice. Oh Andy, it would have been better if you had fallen off the bridge that day when I first began to love you. What did you say? 'Pleasanter ways to d-d-snuff it.'

It was a good audience, already in holiday mood, ready to laugh at anything. Julie Andrews finished with a top A, everyone clapped loudly because she was the only girl in the school learning singing properly, and she was going to be an opera singer. I was already leaning against the French windows in the shadows. The song, thank goodness, was in a low key, so that I'd sound like a very light tenor.

Four bars introduction. At two and a half bars, a split second before the light came up on me, I have to admit I very nearly threw in the towel and fled. Instead I swallowed hard, and began to sing.

I've been cherishing
Through the perishing
Winter nights and days . . .

I heard a rustle go round the hall. Julia told me afterwards that the first impression was that they'd got one of the boys from the school along the road, some new hunk on the scene, until someone whispered, 'It's Alex!' Me, after that first rustle, I heard nothing, not even Lorna singing her part. I was in Andy's bedroom, looking out over the harbour.

We'll watch the whole world pass before us
While we are sitting still
Leaning on our own window sill . . .

There was no question of breaking down or tears or making a fool of myself not finishing the song. I sang it like I never sang before, just for Andy, wherever he was now, and for whatever we might have shared. And I knew the audience, even a lot of adolescent schoolgirls, were with me, because when we finished, there was a little hush before they began clapping. It wasn't much, it was even a little puzzled, but I was satisfied.

I went straight back to the classrooms, not waiting to see the rest of the revue from the wings as all the rest were. Julia, faithfully, was there waiting.

In silence I handed her the suit, which she hung up for me. I took off the shirt and tie, the shoes. Methodically, slowly, with complete control, I removed the make-up, and put my school uniform back on. I think she was quite scared of me at that point. To tell the truth, I was quite scared of me, too.

I went into the cloakroom and got out the bottle of shampoo I'd brought with me. We weren't supposed to use the hot water, but I washed my greasy face and then my greasy hair in the basin. I towelled my hair dry and combed it. 'There,' I said.

'I cried,' said Julia, finally. 'Do you know that, you terrible girl, tears and tears. I stood at the back of the wings because I couldn't bear to look at you. Just your voice . . .'

I didn't want to know. Julia had had a soft spot for Andy, she'd even been out with him once, last year, but this was between Andy and me.

Right now I was going home, I was not waiting for the final curtain call with streamers and three cheers for whoever and could Julia please tell Fish-face that I wasn't feeling well and had gone home.

My first gift to Andy had been delivered. Now I intended to put my heart and soul into the second. As they say, we can do the impossible while you wait. Miracles take a little longer.

*What a fool! I've just remembered, Andy. The race
nearly gone and I've only just flicked up, she can't
see me either. We're both flying blind!*

*That's right, you chump. Don't think you're the
only one with the handicaps. Maggie's frightened out
of her tiny mind.*

She's never.

*This time she is. She knows you've got longer arms
than her. You can lunge for the wall.*

I should take up fencing.

*You could try winning this race first. Ten yards.
The crowd is going wild.*

*I can see them when I turn my head, people on the
side of the pool, arms waving . . .*

*Don't worry about them. Say after me . . . First,
Alexandra Archer . . .*

*First, Alexandra Archer . . . I'm dying, Andy. My
arms are falling off . . . I stopped breathing about a
minute ago.*

13

From the day school finished, three days after the concert, my times started to improve.

We closed the year with the flourish of prize-giving, where Julia and I trooped up far too often: she won all the Fifth Form science prizes, me prizes for English, drama, Latin, music, senior swimming champ, the Fifth Form Belinda Parr Memorial Shield (who was she?) for all-around ability and leadership. I was also mentioned in dispatches by Miss Gillies, best wishes of the school in my quest for Olympic nomination, think of her training while the rest of us are sunbathing . . . Laying it on a bit thick.

Training was still a grind, but it had become a grind with purpose and some of my old pleasure in the feel of the water had come back. I looked forward to training sessions, rather than dreading them, especially the early morning ones with the pool clean and smooth and blue, and only a few people there. Now I trained alone.

Perhaps I'd become some sort of a masochist, or perhaps I'd just been lazy before, but I almost welcomed the pain, the gasping for breath towards the end of a time trial. Mr Jack tried hard to look unimpressed as he checked his stop-watch each time, but the little nod of his head told me he was pleased as he wrote times and heart-rates down in his book and drew curves on various graphs.

I was on an upward curve again. It had been a long time coming.

My second clash with Maggie, the weekend after school finished, was encouraging, too. It was a fine summer night for once. We had two events, two hundred and twenty yards first, then a hundred and ten yard invitation, with the best seniors still around and a couple of promising juniors (I'd been one once), which had been put on late in the programme as the 'highlight' so that people would stay and see us. There'd also been talk that Maggie might be near to a national record, as she'd been edging close to it in training.

Mr Jack had firmly told me just to cruise through the two hundred and twenty yards treating it as a warm-up. Maggie never cruised through anything; she always swam against the clock. So when we turned for the last lap of what I thought had been an easy race, I was astonished to find myself right up with her. Twenty yards from home and we were still together. Ten yards and she had the edge. Five yards and I was not so sure. We touched together, but when the timekeepers and judges had come out of their huddle it was Maggie by point two.

'Nice swim,' said Mr Jack when I'd changed into dry togs and joined him to get instructions for the sprint. Dad, alongside, looked pleased too. 'Looked good, easy. Better than I've seen you for some while.'

'Felt good.' Further down in the enclosure I could

see Maggie with her coach and her mother, heads together. Mr Jack followed my gaze, but did not say anything.

'You can wind it up for the sprint. Go out fast, settle down, throttle back just a bit after the turn, dig in the last half length. Don't expect a miracle. Maggie's exceptionally fit and sharp for so early in the season. *But* . . . I am greatly encouraged, Alex.'

The last time we sat in this same place, less than a month ago, there'd been another person here. I'd been another person then, too: a child who talked too much. Now I knew too much.

By the time the sprint event was due, some forty minutes later, I had run the whole gamut of depression and elation: hope that I just might be able to turn the tables on Maggie and despair that her Aussie training would count in the end. Yet I had her rattled. She kept clear of me as we assembled for the event. She tried the old trick of keeping us all waiting just a little longer than polite, slowly peeling her track suit off, while the rest of us stood by our blocks and shivered. I stood windmilling my arms and smiling. According to the papers, it was she who was supposed to be breaking the record, not me. Her burden. I had enough of my own.

A perfect start, and again I felt good. She was on my left, so I knew that I had edged ahead as we neared the turn, maybe half a yard. A perfect turn; this was all too good to be true. I felt so good I forgot to throttle back. Pain set in, but I felt I was using it to ride the wave, not fight it. I dared not take a right-handed breath to see if I still led, but there was a black shape right up with me. To win this race would put me right back in the picture.

I touched. Maggie touched too, but as I lay back on the ropes I saw my timekeepers straighten up smiling. One old friend gave me the thumbs up. There was a certain amount of commotion around the pool.

'Good swim, Alex,' said Maggie.

'Thanks.' She looked cheerful enough, but I wondered how she felt, really. If anything, she had more at stake and more to lose, publicly anyway.

The announcer's voice came over loud and clear. 'First, Miss A. Archer, swimming for . . .' The rest was lost in cheers. As I climbed out of the pool, an old friend, who'd been standing on the side of the pool as a timekeeper for as long as I could remember, showed me the stop-watch. 'It was sixty-six point three,' she said. 'Only point three off Maggie's record. A grand swim. You deserved that.'

I glowed, I danced back into the changing-room and out to see Dad and Mr Jack. Point three! In all fairness Maggie still had a slightly faster unofficial time and tonight she'd been off form. But I'd proved I could!

I was back in the picture, literally, with both papers splashing headlines and a head-and-shoulders of me. 'MAGGIE BENTON DEFEATED', said one. 'MISS ARCHER WINS', said the other. 'Surprise win to Miss Archer at last night's invitation meeting', 'brilliantly judged race', 'hitting form after a disappointing season', 'fulfilling earlier promise', and 'fine clashes expected at the

Auckland and national championships later in the season'. 'Their rivalry is as intense as that between the great English backstroke swimmers Judy Grinham and Margaret Edwards in recent years,' said one commentator. 'Which of them wins the national titles in February and subsequently the Olympic nomination will be a seasoned and worthy competitor.'

Mr Jack, true to form, didn't go overboard, but I knew he was delighted, behind his warnings that this race was a mere stepping stone, it was the nationals now, less than two months away. A lot of distance had to be clocked up between now and then.

For the first time in my life, I had nothing to do but swim.

That's not strictly true, either. There was Christmas, only a few days away, and New Year. I was spending much more time with my family. Julia was away with her family. When I wasn't at the pool I was at home, helping with Christmas things like making hundreds of mince pies and writing cards, and doing the annual visit to some of Gran's cronies around the place. ('My, what a big girl you've grown,' like Red Riding Hood's wolf.) I looked after the kids while Mum and Gran went shopping. Then Gran looked after them while Mum and I went shopping, or I looked after Gran while Mum took the kids shopping.

Gran had a Christmas rush on with her baby dresses, and helping her in the afternoons between lunch and training gave me the solitude, the time that I needed. We would work in silence, just the sounds of her Singer sewing machine whirring away, the kids playing outside in the tree-hut, flies buzzing in the windows. If Gran noticed that sometimes my hands were still and my eyes wet, she didn't say anything.

I think I began to get a reputation among the swimming crowd for being remote, a bit weird even. It wasn't intentional. I just didn't have much to say to Maggie or anyone these days. The pressure was on her too, with her mother's stop-watch clicking off her time trials and mine too, and engaging her coach in long conversations, while the rest of his squad hung about. I listened to Mr Jack, did my usual, sometimes with the boys in the squad, but usually alone, and went home.

Sometimes I took a book and lay in the sun for half an hour or so after training. But I had to be careful of sunburn, of peeling and blisters, which chafing togs could turn to sores. And the image of Andy was still too vivid; every time I walked through the ticket office I thought of him, saw his long frame leaning against the rail around the pool, waiting for me. Every time I stood on the block, psyching myself up for yet another three miles, his long shape was there in the water. When I lay on the terrace I heard his voice, remembered our rare kisses when no one was around, still so recent. Tears came then, too. For the first time in my life, despite all my family and easy friendships among the swimming crowd, I felt like someone separate. Last. Loneliest.

Christmas Day dawned brilliantly. Although the pool didn't open until mid-morning, I woke early anyway and joined the kids tearing their Christmas stockings to pieces. We found all sorts of tiny goodies, sweeties, cherries, grapes, and an orange in the toe, which Gran told us, every Christmas, was an English custom going back to the time when an orange was an incredible treat, imported at great expense from Spain or Italy. 'You kids in this land of fruit, you don't know what it's like to taste one orange, the only fresh fruit through an entire English winter. My mother knew, before she emigrated out here.'

Mid-morning it was church. As a family we went only at Christmas and Easter, and for what Mum called 'Hatches, Matches and Dispatches', which I suppose is better than not at all. Gold, yellow and white flowers were everywhere, and ladies in hats, and the long service was made longer by much hearty singing of carols. Twenty days since I last sat in a church; and there were still tears left inside me.

Home to help Mum and Gran prepare the turkey; the table set with holly and pohutukawa flowers picked from the old tree in the garden, colour scheme of green and crimson and white. Lunch went on for ages, with far too much to eat and toasts to all, and Gran raising her glass to 'absent loved ones and friends'. She meant mostly grandfather Albert, who'd gone under to drink and the Depression, and Dad's parents who lived down south, but I saw Mum look at me and raise her glass.

After all the presents were opened, and tables cleared and dishes washed and kids shooed out to the garden, Dad and I got in the car. Dad hesitated before he turned the starter.

'You're sure . . . ?'

'They're expecting me. I rang a few days ago and asked when they'd like me to visit, if at all. Mrs Richmond said come Christmas Day, for afternoon tea.'

'That was thoughtful of you, Alex.'

It had cost me something, to ring up Andy's mother and find out that no, they were not going away, and yes, they'd like me to call around four on Christmas Day.

'How long do you want?' said Dad as he pulled up outside the house.

'Maybe half an hour. I'll walk down to the beach.'

'Outside the dairy then, half past? I'll wait.'

'Thanks, Dad.' I pushed the car door shut. I'd eaten too much but that was probably not the only reason I was feeling slightly ill.

The house had a closed-up look. Venetian blinds down, garage door shut. Even the door chime sounded muffled.

Mrs Richmond opened the door so smartly that I knew she'd been watching out for me. 'Come in, dear.'

How can you say happy Christmas? I said nothing but hello. Besides she looked awful, I was shocked. She'd become a little old lady, still upright, carefully dressed in powder blue twinsets, but haggard. Less prim people might have wanted a comforting hug, but I was wary and she held out a formal hand to shake. 'Come in, come in.'

I followed her into the darkened living-room. The View from this Room was shut out by blinds. Mr Richmond rose from a leather chair and greeted me equally formally. I handed over the small present of chocolates I'd brought with me.

'Alex, good to see you. Sit down, please.'

There was a slight awkward silence. Then I thought this is not on, I'm doing to them what other people have done to me, hiding their embarrassment behind silence, dodging the issue. I took a deep breath.

'I wanted to tell you . . . that I've been thinking of Andy, and of you, since . . . You probably know I'm not a very religious person, but in church this morning I said some prayers. Some of them were for you, because I just can't imagine what it would be like . . . And worse at Christmas, with everyone's little kids pulling crackers and opening presents, all the talk of babies being born and goodwill and stuff . . . Anyway, I prayed.'

Mrs Richmond was sitting primly as usual, looking at her feet. The trolley beside her chair was beautifully set for tea and covered with a flimsy embroidered throw-over thing.

Mr Richmond spoke first, with just the hint of a smile on his face. 'Thank you, dear, for your prayers. We need all the help we can get. It has not been easy.'

'Christmas is a sham,' said Mrs Richmond suddenly. 'We've just had Christmas dinner with my sister and her husband, their children of course are grown and overseas. Kind of them, I know, to make the effort, but . . .'

She stood up abruptly. 'Would you like tea, Alex?'

'Yes. Yes, please.'

Mr Richmond watched her leave, and took refuge in stoking his pipe up. 'Very hard for her, all this. Andrew was her whole life.'

I heard myself say, 'Funny how people don't say anything. Your boyfriend gets killed and they talk about the weather.'

'Embarrassment. Fear of saying the wrong thing, making it worse.' He took a deep puff of his pipe and looked hard at me. 'You had more than a soft spot for our Andrew, didn't you?'

'I suppose . . . more than.' Some loyalty to Andy prevented me from saying we had an agreement to wait for each other, a sort of engagement.

He nodded, almost as though he'd read my mind. 'You'd have been good for him, too. You've a streak of ambition, a toughness that he lacked.'

Ambition for his goals, or his father's? What do I say? Rightly or wrongly, I decided what was the point, a sad father should keep his dream, so I said only, 'He knew what he wanted. And we were good for each other.'

Mrs Richmond returned with a magnificent silver teapot. I was getting the favoured nation treatment. The conversation turned to my swimming, my win against Maggie, my hopes for Rome. I was offered asparagus sandwiches and home-baked afghans. After I turned down a third cup of tea, Mrs Richmond said, 'Please could you come, Alex. I have something . . .'

I followed her, along the corridor to the closed door of Andy's bedroom. She stood for a moment, then slowly opened the door. 'Please . . .' Her gesture indicated that I was to go in first.

I was none too keen, but I had no choice. The curtains were still drawn and there was an unlived-in smell, musty, slightly old socks. When my eyes got used to the gloom I saw that nothing had been touched since my first visit, right down to the wet towel on the floor.

'I haven't been in here since the night he died,' she said softly behind me. I said nothing, what on earth could I say. I thought of taking her hand, but when I turned to look at her, I saw only the impassive face of a woman who'd hidden her feelings all her life. So now she stood with blank face, while God knows what went on in her mind. I might have been the only person whose shoulder she could cry on, but for her it was too late.

We stood there for maybe a minute, although it seemed like an hour. 'Thank you, dear,' she said, moving to close the door. 'Clearing out the room is something I was dreading. Coming with you has helped.' She might have been talking about having to do a spot of spring-cleaning.

'Could I help?' I longed to fling wide the curtains, take my last look at Our View.

'No, thank you, dear. It's my job and I'll do it in a day or so.'

She will too, with her back upright and her heart broken into tiny pieces; tidily and methodically, till not a trace remains of the person that Andy had been. All his dreams, in cardboard boxes. I needed fresh air.

Mr Richmond met us in the hallway. I thought it was a good moment to leave, but as I started to speak Mrs Richmond interrupted me.

'Just a moment, Alex. I'd like you to have . . .' I didn't hear the rest, because she was walking back down to Andy's room. She went in without hesitation this time, and a few seconds later came out carrying the large transistor radio, which she held out to me without a word. I wasn't sure what she meant.

'Andrew would have liked you to have this.'

'Oh no, I couldn't . . .'

'Please, he would . . .'

'It's very kind, but . . .'

'He treasured it.'

Mr Richmond said, 'Alex, please. He worked hard for that, driving a van for the local grocer after school.'

Something I hadn't known. And you say he lacked ambition, drive, I thought. Not him.

'Well, I . . . shall treasure it too,' I said. I had to get out, and quickly. 'Please, I must go . . . Dad's waiting . . . Um, goodbye . . . Thank you . . .'

To my departing back, Mrs Richmond called, 'Come and see us again, Alex. When you're passing . . . ?'

It wasn't a very gracious exit. I turned at the bottom of the steps and waved. They were standing in the porch, each in a separate space. I almost ran down to the beach, although the transistor was quite heavy and I didn't want to bang it on anything. It was inside the half hour, but Dad was waiting. I put the radio on the back seat, and climbed in the car.

'What's that?'

'His mother gave it to me.'

Dad just nodded wisely. I didn't feel very wise about anything. We drove to the pool in silence, for which I was grateful. 'I'll put it in your room. Do you want picking up later?'

'I'll walk.' It was a fair distance home, but I needed time to myself. I was beginning to need the isolation of training, just me and the water and the black lines on the bottom of the pool, back and forth. That Christmas afternoon I discovered you could cry and swim at the same time, and no one would know. A pale face and blood-shot eyes they'd put down to swimming pools and hard work.

From Boxing Day the days started to wash into each other. I hardly knew what day of the week it was. New Year's Eve came and went. I turned down a party with some of Mr Jack's squad, and Mum let me off the family affair after the barbecue in the garden when all the kids played spotlight with torches and insisted on staying up until midnight.

I went to bed early and heard nothing. Sleep was coming easier these nights as the nightmares were less frequent and I was physically so tired, clocking up between four and five miles a day if you added my two sessions together, plus weights and forty minutes' calisthenics.

The Auckland champs in the second week of January attracted a lot of interest because apart from Maggie and me there were others, especially a couple of boys, with hopes for the Games team. But the weather was pretty terrible for mid-January, with a nasty wind turning all the swimmers blue and blowing up the skirts and raincoats of the women officials stoically doing their jobs night after night at the end of the pool.

Times were slow. The press tried to turn my races with Maggie into great clashes. I tried hard, and there was less than point seven in all the events, but there were too many events, what with heats and finals, and club relays, and I didn't try my hardest, not really. Mr Jack didn't *quite* tell me to be happy for once with silvers, but that was what he wanted, too: to lull Maggie into a false sense of security. So I read the headlines in her favour with hardly a twinge. And there were some promising juniors, particularly a young man brilliant at the new dolphin butterfly, who threatened to steal the limelight as we had once done. Good for them!

24 January, and the dreaded letter was sitting on my bed when I got home from training. Julia had already rung to say she was coming round at eleven, but she wouldn't tell Mum what she'd got. I shut the door and slowly opened the envelope.

English 88. History, well well, 74. Latin 68 (not bad for a terrible paper). Maths 79 (surprise, surprise). And Music 91 (and so I should, after all that piano theory).

Not bad, all things considered. Yes, I'm pleased, I decided. Family were very pleased. Mr Jack when I saw him later at the pool was pleased. I sent a little message to Andy. He was pleased, too. But Julia bounced in the door ecstatic.

'Tell me.' She'd done it, it was only a question of by how much.

'My top four—three hundred and seventy-two.'

I realized I'd forgotten how to laugh, to cry for pleasure, to shout for joy.

'Three hundred and seventy-two—for *four* subjects?'

'Yes.'

We danced, yelled, shrieked around the kitchen. Mum and Dad, who knew nothing of Julia's situation, thought we'd gone mad and all the kids came rushing in to see what the commotion was.

Later, in my bedroom, I said, 'What did your father say? That's better than either of your brothers.'

'Funny, you know, he was actually quite pleased, although *they* weren't. He's started telling all and sundry, "My clever daughter, brilliant at science you know, is going to do medicine." Em-*barra*-ssing!'

'The old rogue. Well, he just had to get used to the idea, didn't he?' I hadn't felt so warm inside for months. Julia was walking on air, brown as a berry after her holiday, the dark shadows under her eyes as faint as I'd seen them in years. 'Oh, I'm happy for you,' I said, giving her a bear hug.

'How are *you*, Alex? You've got an awfully lean and hungry look about you. And dangerous. Maggie, watch out. How's . . . the other thing?'

'All right. No, it's not all right. I think too much. But I don't feel so angry now, just . . . sort of grim. Dangerous, if you like.' I also said it lightly, but it wasn't a bad word to describe how I felt these days.

A couple of days later I got a strange phone call from Mrs Richmond, which had me right back to anger and anguish, weeping on my bed for a long while, banging my fists against the pillow at the cruelty, the unfairness, the waste, and my loneliness. She thought I'd like to know that Andy's scholarship results had just arrived in the mail. Somehow, someone had boobed; it had not got through to Wellington, what had happened. He'd gained excellent marks in maths, biology, geography, physics and chemistry and won a National Junior Scholarship.

First, Alexandra Archer. Second, Alexandra Archer. Ninety-fifth, Alexandra Archer . . . Also ran, Alexandra Archer . . . Go, Alex, Alex, go . . .

You can hear the crowd, Alex? It's pandemonium down there, Alex. Your father's on his feet, Gran's actually standing on the bench, jumping up and down, Mr Jack is still sitting on his butt biting the quicks of his nails. He can't bear to look.

I bet Mrs Benton can't either.

She's gone very pale. The Aussie coach beside her has just said something about that Archer girl's got courage, great fighter, and she's just bit his head off. He's come right back at her and says he knows real talent and spirit when he sees it, and Mrs Benton thinks he's getting at Maggie, putting her down, and no one's ever done that, ever, and for once in her life she's speechless.

Serve the woman right. Though not fair to Maggie.

Maggie's scared out of her brain. Not really of losing to you. She's got a lot of time for you . . .

It's mutual.

Her mother's face. Disapproval, disappointment,

written all over. That's what Maggie's afraid of, guilt, letting her mother down. It's going to take her another whole year to come to terms with it, not until . . . No, I mustn't say that, not yet.

I've beaten her before . . .

This time is special. It has become more than just a swimming race to you. Why else are you pushing yourself past your limit . . .

True. Oh Andy, when will it end . . .

You're doing well. Courage . . .

14

'You'll do it' said Mum as we hugged out by the car. 'It's written in your stars, in your eyes.' She had tears in hers, Mum the serene, the unflappable, the big strong nurse whose shoulder everyone else cried on. 'I'll be listening to the radio, but ring me anyway, each night.'

Gran did the kissing rounds too, just as wound up as I was, in her way. First time back to Napier in fifteen years, so naturally she was excited. She'd come up to help Mum when I was born (Dad had gone back to his ship and the war), and somehow, apart from going back for a few weeks to sell her tiny flat, had just stayed.

During family talk at tea about Napier one night, I'd suddenly thought, why isn't she coming with us? Because she couldn't, she said when I asked her later; couldn't leave Mum, leave the kids, she had too many baby dress orders to meet, and anyway where would she stay. Haven't you friends? 'They're all dead or moved away,' she said, adding, 'I suppose there might be old Lillian,' and I caught a whiff of longing before she closed the conversation.

The real reason, of course, was money. She hated getting presents, new clothes, anything spent on her. She'd no more listen to Mum and Dad than she would to me, except perhaps . . . So I drew some money out of my savings account and bailed her up in her room. 'For you, for Napier,' I said firmly, closing her hand around the notes.

'You can't do that.'

'I can and I have. I don't care whether you use it to stay in a hotel, or with old Lillian or whatever. It's yours.'

'I can't possibly . . .'

'Oh yes you can. Look at me.' The tough old warrior's eyes were glinting, with hope as well as tears. 'You can, Gran. You've been helping me, all of us, for years and it's about time you had a holiday.'

'I don't need holi . . .'

'We all need holidays. Gran, if you don't come, I shall be personally hurt, offended, rejected . . .' She looked up to see whether I was serious or joking. I was both. It was a mean trick, but it worked. We spoke the same language, Gran and I. 'Do you want me just to mention it to Dad, casual-like? You'd rather like to go back to your old haunts?'

It took a lot to silence Gran. She nodded, and busied herself at her sewing machine because she thought that way I'd not see how moved she was.

I lost the battle over the front seat of the car, though. When I opened the door for her, she simply climbed in the back, and smiled triumphantly. 'Drive carefully, Jim,' called Mum through the open window.

We waved to the farewell committee as Dad backed down the drive. The brats, still with breakfast Marmite on their faces, were all yelling 'Good luck,

Alex,' as they followed the car and chased us along the street. It was Saturday morning, and I'd already done my two miles. Dad had taken a whole week's leave. I had special permission to travel down with him, rather than in the team bus, which was also leaving this morning but would take much longer.

I hadn't ever swum in Napier. Down the Great South Road Gran talked darkly of the road between Taupo and Napier. 'Fit only for mules. Our radiators used to boil, so we'd have to stop half-way up and wait for an hour.' 'But that was the 1920s, Gran,' I said. 'You were driving an old jalopy. A 1956 Morris Oxford, surely . . .' 'You wait.'

By the time we got to Taupo five hours later, I was almost past caring. Dad drove slowly and the un-sealed bits of road through the forests slowed us down, too. We had Mum's bacon and egg pie and thermos tea in Taupo, on the edge of the lake, after a gorgeous swim in the cleanest, purest water I have ever seen. I didn't swim any distance, maybe a quarter of a mile out into the lake over neat rippling ridges of white sand.

Although the schools had been back a week, there was a holiday atmosphere here, with lots of children in the shallows, and people my age fooling around and diving off a raft moored about a pool's length offshore. We sat in silence watching them.

Dad said, 'You've forgotten what it's like, haven't you?'

'What?'

'To frolic like that. Carefree, no stop-watch. You

go for a swim and it's a training session, half-way out into the lake.'

'A measly quarter mile?' I lay back on the hot sand.

'All this striving, driving, I sometimes wonder where my little daughter has gone.'

There was a long silence. 'And what about the wolf whistles?' he said, teasing.

'Dad!' As if it mattered, now. The sleek fit, the vivid emerald colour of my one decent pair of togs made a change from boring black racers. If grinning lads can think of nothing better to do than lie around and gawk . . .

Below us on the water's edge a tall guy was rigging his yacht. Both boat and figure not unlike, if I half shut my eyes . . . If, if! I knew that poem of Kipling's. Apart from the 'You'll be a Man, my son!' bit, it was something to hold on to.

If you can make one heap of all your winnings
And risk it on one turn of pitch-and-toss,
And lose, and start again . . .

Dad was talking. 'Alex, I want you to know . . . Whatever happens, I'll be proud of you.'

Not knowing what to say, I nodded.

'You've come through these past months . . . I haven't said much (he never does, Dad), but I've watched. I'm proud of you already.'

Gran's hand, on my other side, took mine and squeezed hard.

'She'll do it, our Alex,' she said. 'I know she will.'

'Time to go,' said Dad. I never did see the full extent of Gran's dark hills on the Taupo-Napier road. Warmed by the sun, and lulled by the slow rhythm of the car around bend after bend, twisting and turning at ten miles per hour, I slept all the way to Napier.

We arrived at dusk, just as they turned the lights of the Marine Parade on, and drove slowly past a skating rink, sound shell, gardens, statues, aquarium, lamps reflected in small pools, and that mighty row of Norfolk pines you see in every picture of Napier. Behind was the beach, strictly scenic, with dangerous Pacific dumpers crashing noisily down on to stones.

On a warm Saturday night, people were out and about; crowds of teenagers, some fairly ordinary, others in big American cars, were heading to Saturday night flicks. Right up one end of the beach, near the port, almost under the headland, Gran pointed out the pool. It was closed. Posters, here and elsewhere in the city, proclaimed the New Zealand Swimming Championships. 'See our Olympic prospects compete for nomination: Maggie Benton, Alexandra Archer . . .'

Dad saw me into my room at the team hotel, only a street away from the pool. 'You're room seven, with a Miss Davidson,' said the woman at the desk downstairs. 'Originally it was a Miss Benton, but her mother insisted she go in the suite with her. They

227

arrived two days ago, such a nice girl. I keep reading about her in the papers. I imagine you know her quite well.'

'Quite well.' From her slight sniff I could imagine what had happened. Dad was smiling, too.

'And just as well,' Dad said as we humped my bags up the stairs. 'For once I agree. The officials who did the allocations must be out of their minds. Hopeless!'

'Oh, I don't know.' But Carol Davidson was OK. She was a breaststroker, a race apart.

It was another room with a view—across roof-tops to the Norfolk pines and the ocean beyond. I hardly heard Dad as I stood at the window, remembering another room.

'You'll be all right then?'

'What? Oh, yes, 'course. Thanks, Dad,' as he kissed me goodnight. 'Hope your place is OK. Look after Gran.'

Dad, after that long drive, looked tired, too. 'See you at nine, at the pool.'

I fell into bed and surprisingly, despite sitting in a car all day, slid straight into sleep. Around eleven the team bus arrived and I heard people finding rooms. As she threw herself into bed, Carol muttered something about a puncture and never wanting to see another hill in her life. After that I kept waking, tossing on the bed, which was too narrow and too soft, dreaming of waves falling, trees falling, a yacht, a bike, a boy falling, myself falling, swimming through air, falling, in lazy floating slow-motion, always downwards like the regular thud of the breakers along the nearby beach.

*　*　*

Sunday, Monday, only light training now, a mile or so, tapering off, with lots of sprints, starting practice, turns until my head was full of water. Hundreds of competitors jostling for pool space, stop-watches, coaches, reporters, parents' gossip and predictions. Dad and Mr Jack watched my training from the back of the stands, quietly avoiding the general team activity. Mrs Benton sat by herself on the other side.

I knew my new reputation: iceberg, unforthcoming, unfriendly, crazy, gone a bit odd. Juniors kept clear. So did Maggie. Officials didn't stop me for chats as they'd once done and reporters got the cold shoulder. I was having only three or four hours' sleep a night, yet I felt as fit as I'd ever done, hungry, lean and, yes, dangerous.

Tuesday, opening night, and Maggie won the four hundred and forty yards, by point seven. It was my worst event, and the one I least expected to win, but Thursday I knew I *had* to win the two hundred and twenty yards to remain in the hunt for Rome. For the freestyle crown it was best of three.

I swam the race according to Mr Jack's instructions; feeling good, I knew from the start I could do it. The last lap was the hardest I'd ever swum. Maggie was on my breathing side. She didn't yield an inch, and at the end there was only point four in it. But I knew I had won. It was a national record, two minutes twenty-three point one seconds. One each. As we heard the result in the pool, Maggie gave me a hug and we both grinned for the photographers. The smiles on Mr Jack's moonface and Dad's cragface were worth every last gasp. As for Gran, her little back was ramrod straight.

But there was the first hint of the price I had to pay, the forthcoming game. Leaving the pool at the end of the night, Mrs Benton (never mind, 'Congratulations, Alex') walked straight past me in the foyer, and again in the hotel dining-room. OK, I thought, I'm invisible. Watch me win an invisible gold. Play rough.

I put a call through to Mum and heard general family jubilation, whoops and cries, at the other end. They'd all been listening to the radio. It was a good feeling, and so was reading the paper the next morning, until I got to the bit about predictions for the sprint title. 'Miss Benton, because of her greater consistency over the past four seasons, must start as the favourite.'

The very thought of Saturday sent shivers up and down my spine. I would have only one chance, like a singer having to hit a stupendous top note without cracking or the ballerina doing the Rose Adagio in *Sleeping Beauty* and holding her *attitude* on one pointe for many breath-taking seconds. She couldn't wobble over and then say to the audience, 'I'm sorry, I'll do that again.'

The performer has one chance. One heap of all her winnings . . .

Friday, for me a rest day. Dad, Gran and I went to visit some relatives in Hastings for lunch. Dad thought, Mr Jack thought, and I agreed that I needed to get away for a few hours after training in the morning. I got special permission from our team manager Mr Upjohn, and the chaperone Mrs Hooper, who seemed to be having a few problems keeping track of one particular sixteen-year-old with a mind of her own. I hardly remember a thing about the visit: the family, the house, the lunch, the countryside, anything. Does that sound crazy? But I *was* crazy by now, obsessed with that unforgiving minute that lay ahead.

Five yards Alex. Maggie's as desperate as you are. Her stroke has disintegrated a bit. Her mother is frozen, still as a stone, white-faced. She thinks it's all over.

My stroke went out the window ages ago. I feel like some sort of crazy windmill.

Looks good to me. I've always loved watching you swim, Alex, the sheer power of you. I get the same feeling watching dolphins in the sea out from the beach.

I was thinking of dolphins earlier.

Wait till afterwards, concentrate on what you're doing. Three yards, Alex, she thinks she's got you . . .

Andy, help me, please . . . I want, so badly . . . to win.

15

I didn't go to the Friday evening session to cheer
Carol and the other Aucklanders on. Neither did
Maggie, and I think most of the other people in the
team understood why, although one or two eyebrows
were raised, notably Mr Upjohn when I told him I
wanted to get an early night. He said of course Alex,
but his eyes gave me another message. You could
always tell those officials who'd been competitors
themselves, or who had children of their own com-
peting. He had neither. I'd heard Dad say he'd come
in the side door, to improve administration.

After tea, in that same cool hour before dusk as the
night we'd arrived, Dad, Gran and I went for a walk
along the Marine Parade. We wandered through the
gardens without talking much, and read the legend
of Pania under the bronze statue. Sitting, smiling
Pania of the Reef, sea-woman, part-taniwha, married
to human Karetaki but drawn back to the sea to live
with her family. Many people had been drawn, as I
was now, to stroke the smooth polished bronze. Her
limbs were full and strong. Give me some of your
strength, Pania. Already I had the sinking feeling in
my stomach and still there was a whole night and day
to survive.

* * *

Carol had promised not to wake me when she came in, but she needn't have worried. I'd gone to bed at nine thirty, and ninety minutes and almost a whole book later I was still wide awake.

'Silver! Look.' She held up the medal, delighted with herself. She had hardly dared hope for the bronze, and had swum two seconds faster than her own personal best. I sat up, shared her joy, and heard other fates and fortunes. Then I must have yawned. 'Hell, I'm sorry, Alex, you're all wide awake now.'

'I was wide awake before,' I said. I was beginning to have a very unwelcome suspicion. It was another ten minutes before I could bring myself to get out of bed and investigate.

'Oh no, no! Damn, damn, damn.'

'What's the matter?' When I didn't reply she said sharply. 'Alex?'

I came out of the bathroom. 'My period, a whole week early. I haven't even brought any . . .'

'Here.' She rummaged around in her suitcase. 'Stress, I suppose. Don't you take those pills? In our squad, we all do.'

'My coach reckons there's no proof that you go slower with a period. I've swum good times with and without it. So why upset all your hormones? He doesn't go for pills.'

'Not even vitamins? Everyone does that. The Aussies eat them like sweeties, by the ton so they say.'

'Sure, that's different.'

'There's a rumour going around, pep pills, some of the guys from . . .

'Carol, please can I go to sleep? Thanks for the doings.' I turned my back on her. I didn't want to hear about whoever might be taking pep pills because that was just plain stupid, as well as illegal. We'd heard enough from overseas to know that pep pills sent you all the way up and then crashing all the way down, and in the long run did a lot of harm.

But I was not nearly as sure about periods affecting your times as I'd sounded. Damn, damn! It was a complication I didn't need. But not an excuse either. I decided not to tell anyone, not Dad or Mr Jack, who always knew my monthly cycle exactly. There'd be no excuses, no justifications, no complications, if I could help it.

Fate had other things in store. Carol finally got to bed, turned her light out, I suppose about eleven thirty. I willed my eyes to close, willed myself to sleep. It was a warm night, and I seemed to be either too hot under one blanket or not quite warm enough with just a sheet. I heard the breakers' regular drumbeat, a distant clock strike midnight, and some more people (adults) walk along the corridor outside and say noisy goodnights and bang their doors shut.

Then I must have slipped into a sort of sleep for a few minutes before I was standing on a starting-block, then swimming around in the sea and between me and the shore was this gigantic surf, not the rolling kind which you could, with luck, ride to safety, but the evil dumping kind, which makes a point of hurling its victims head-first into the sand, breaking every bone before washing your body ashore, and now I have to choose between the surf and a school of sharks, I am Tinman again, crumpled silver tossed ashore, but look what else the surf throws up on to the moonlit sand, Miss Macrae in full costume as a witch from *Macbeth*, with blacked-out teeth, more skull than face, Andy in school uniform, but covered with blood and his handsome face set in a smiling death mask, terrifying in its smoothness and perfection, and a female body, broken and twisted by the force of the sea, which I recognize as myself . . .

I sat up in bed, rigid. Carol told me in the morning she'd heard me cry out in my sleep, a loud wail that had penetrated down to her marrow. Slowly the images, so dreadfully clear, faded. I got out of bed and stood, shivering, sweating, at the open window. The street below was deserted and most of the lights along Marine Parade out. I could hear the crash of those breakers on the beach, and a persistent song in my head.

A room with a view—and you,
With no one to worry us,
No one to hurry us—through
This dream we've found . . .

Some dream! I had a snowflake's chance of sleeping. If I thought backwards, the dream, its waves, its vision of death, would overwhelm me again, and next time it would be worse. If I thought forwards, it was to tomorrow's task, just a swimming race, for heaven's sake, and yet so much more than that. I had to concentrate on the present to stay sane. Carol, although she'd been stirring when I woke, was back out for the count, silver-satisfied, snoring lightly. I knew I either had to go for a swim or go mad. I needed water to clean my mind, and stretch my aching body.

I put my track suit on over my pyjamas, and unhooked a pair of old racers and a towel from the clothes-line we'd rigged up by the window. My sandals made a flip-flop noise, so I carried them. In my very peculiar state, I had no idea where I could swim, but I just had to get my body into water somehow and feel the rhythm of the stroke that had carried me over so many thousands of miles over the years. It might have to be, it could surely not be, the sea . . .

I was cunning enough to remember to snib the door so that it wouldn't lock behind me, and to take some considerable time to creep down the wooden stairs and open the main door. The night wasn't cold, but how I shivered. I walked straight down to the beach. There wasn't a soul around. I sang silently, for some comfort . . .

> . . . *high above the mountains and sea.*
> *We'll bill and we'll coo—ooo-oo,*
> *And sorow will never come,*
> *Oh, will it ever come . . .*

No use going to the pool, Alex. That will be shut.

It took all my resolve to walk through the gardens and on to the shingle, to confront the merciful emptiness of those breakers. I knew as I sat there that I had too much sense to swim alone, now or at any time. My nightmare had been true in one respect: those waves were short, nasty killers. That was why there was a pool right by the beach. 'SWIMMER DROWNS ON EVE OF BIG RACE—The body of Miss Alexandra Archer, strong contender for Olympic swimming nomination, was found on the Napier foreshore this morning. Police say there are no suspicious circumstances . . .' It would look like I'd cracked up under the strain. I couldn't do that to my family. To Mr Jack, whose tubby chubby face when I won the two hundred and twenty yards had been wonderful to behold. Nor to Maggie either. And not to Andy, up? out? there beyond the horizon.

Perhaps there was a way. I sat, trying to blot out the vision of waves and death with the more obvious and very beautiful image before me of a full moon reflected on the water. Nothing but ocean between me and South America. Perhaps . . . I was unhinged enough to consider climbing over something to get into the pool. I began to walk along the beach.

Then a car drove along the road. I stopped and hid in a shadow, needlessly, I suppose since my track suit was dark blue. The car stopped, too, outside the pool. I crept on to the grass skirting along the walls of the pool building, furtive as a cop peering melodramatically around corners in a gangster film.

Whoever had got out of the car had gone inside the pool's main office, and turned a light on. That meant someone with a key, some person who might let me have a dip.

I walked quickly towards the main door, and peered inside. A man in a blazer was standing behind the counter, busy with something.

'Um . . . Excuse me.'

He jumped a mile. 'Who's that?' He thought I was a burglar or something.

'Um . . . Excuse me. Could you—would it be possible . . . ?' You idiot, Alex, of course he'll say no. And then where will you be? Some further native cunning made me stop talking and walk quite boldly into the foyer.

With the light behind him, I could only see that he was about Dad's age, neatly dressed in blazer and tie. I recognized him as the pool manager, usually behind the counter when we arrived at the pool each morning. I'd heard he'd been a good swimmer in his time. He was still fit looking, good-looking, not one of those who'd gone to seed. Surely he'd recognize a damsel in distress. He certainly identified me smartly enough.

'Alex Archer, isn't it?'

'Yes, um . . .'

'What are you wandering around for, this time of night? Don't you see enough of pools? You should be in bed asleep.'

'I should. But I can't.' I must have sounded pretty desperate.

'Nerves? Your big race is tomorrow night. Well, tonight, actually. Stage fright, can't sleep?' He looked hard at me. 'You're not sick, are you? Fever? Do you want me to call a doctor?'

'No, it's just . . . nerves. Bad dreams. Please, I've got my togs. Can you let me have a swim? Just a short one, five minutes?'

He finished whatever he was doing in the drawer. 'I'm not usually here this time of night, you know. I was on my way home from the officials' do at the hotel in town.'

We'd heard, over the years, about the officials' get-togethers. That explained the banging doors after midnight at the hotel.

'Please.'

'I'd a funny feeling I'd not locked up the till properly.'

'Please. Two minutes.'

'Go on then,' he said gruffly. 'But it'll have to be in the dark. I don't want the police over here.'

'I don't mind,' I said, already half-way through the pool entrance. I changed in the shadows in about ten seconds, ran along to the starting end and dived into the blackness.

I've never swum in the dark before or since. But I knew as soon as I hit the water it was the right thing for me, that night. After two laps I felt cleaned out; the pounding of my heart and dreaded pictures in my head had gone. I thought only of my body and its power through the water, the rhythm of my stroke, which was so ingrained into every cell of me. Half of the pool was in shadow, the other in moonlight; I swam in and out of moonbeams.

I knew he was watching me. After six lengths it

occurred to me that he'd be wanting some sleep too, with the pool open for training at six and heats at nine-thirty. I could have gone on for miles. I saw Andy clearly now, his face relaxed and brown, smiling down at me as he had that day on the headland.

Behind a stairway, I put my pyjamas back on, and track suit, and wrapped the towel around my head like a turban.

'Thanks.'

'Thanks for the demo. Before, you looked like being at the end of your tether. In there, you swim like a mermaid. Feel better now?'

'Much.'

'What would you have done if I hadn't happened to be here?'

'I don't know. Climbed over the wall, probably. No one would ever have known.'

'Risky.'

'Yes.'

'Your big race, I've got my money on you after that two hundred and twenty yesterday.'

'Thanks.'

'Sometimes I'm glad my own kids don't want to get into this game. One's seven, full of beans, hasn't learnt to breathe yet, but she can go. You'd be surprised what I see here from my office.'

I thought of Maggie, and others. 'No, I wouldn't.'

'Yourself? Who pushes you—parents, coach, club, press, peer group?'

'Not my parents. They've never pushed me. Or Mr Jack.'

'OK, OK. Bill Jack's a nice bloke.'

'I push myself.'

'I believe you. Well, it's getting late. I'll run you back to your motel.'

'It's only one street away.'

'Can't have girls wandering around . . .'

'I'd rather walk.'

'I insist. What if you got set upon between here and the motel? Good-looking wench like you. I'd be for the high jump. Your Mr Upjohn'd have my guts for garters.'

He didn't mean it, but I was now starting to imagine things, quite unfairly, and those things included not getting in his car. So I took off, running in my bare feet.

I was back at the motel driveway before I heard the car engine. From the safety of the gate I saw him cruise past, no doubt checking that I was safely home. He waved and decided to give a little toot.

Two yards, Alex. There's nothing in it, nothing. You just need a fingernail that's all. Oh, Alex, stretch, reach . . .

God's teeth, Andy . . .

For me . . .

I'm dead, Andy. I have nothing left.

You have, a fingernail, that's all you need . . .

I haven't even got that. I bit them all off years ago. You know how awful my nails are . . .

For God's sake, shut up. You are so near a record, over a second off.

You're kidding me again.

Listen, woman, would I lie?

I've shot my bolt . . .

Don't be crude. Just throw yourself at the wall . . .

What do you think I'm doing?

Reach for a star, Alex. The one I'm holding out . . . The gold one with a record and Rome written on it . . .

16

One thing I learnt during the events of that day: apparently sensible people will believe anything they're told. They won't or don't want to stop and say, 'Hey, wait a minute, is this what it seems?' They jump right in the cactus to conclusions.

In my innocence, feeling relaxed after my moonlit swim, I had crept in the hotel front door, shut it with great care and silence, tiptoed up the stairs and into room seven. What I didn't know, until later when I sorted it all out with Maggie, was that her mother couldn't sleep either. She'd got up and was walking around the room having a cigarette when she heard the car toot. So she looked out the window and under the street light saw me running in the driveway with my hair all bedraggled, saw the car and a person wave in a friendly fashion and drive off. What's more, the toot had woken Maggie, also sleeping only lightly.

At breakfast, over the far side of the dining-room, I saw Mr Upjohn and Mrs Hooper in deep discussion. I was feeling terrible, because with wet hair it had still taken me ages to get to sleep and then I'd woken at the crack of dawn with my heart pounding. But at least I hadn't been carted away screaming, which is what might have happened.

I'd tried to read, got up, went for a walk down to the beach to watch the sun rise out of the sea, and came back to breakfast as soon as the dining-room was open. My heat was early in the programme, so I wanted to get my food down, my body in good working order.

Dad and Gran came in shortly after breakfast. 'You look pale, Alex. How did you sleep?' 'Not so bad.' I wasn't going to tell them, was I, or about the ache in my tum, which could have been nerves or an unusual period pain. We walked over to the pool.

'Good morning, Miss Archer,' said the man behind the counter, with a tactless wink. 'How are we today?' he said, staring hard, so that I frowned, and mumbled, 'Fine, thanks.' He didn't look too good on four hours' sleep either. Dad, thankfully, was preoccupied with getting money out of his wallet. But Mrs Benton standing there in the foyer, she noticed the wink, and the long steady gaze, as I later discovered. The smile on her face should have been a warning to me.

In broad daylight, the pool looked quite inviting. Only a few early-birds were already in. I wanted plenty of time to warm up, time for a few slow lengths to settle my stomach and some sharp sprints to get my arms going. Mr Jack was there. If he looked concerned at my pale face, or the fact that out of the blue he'd been summoned to an urgent meeting with Mr Upjohn up in the committee room, he didn't show it. Today he was all optimism and Aussie good humour.

I did my warm-up, changed into second best togs

as if in a dream. I sat with Dad and Gran for a while, and then went and found a distant spot in the competitors' enclosure. I was avoiding Maggie, and she me.

Ten minutes before the session was due to begin, I saw Mr Jack come back and join Dad. Then a reporter, a young guy from one of the bigger papers, came over. He was new to the game this season, but had seemed friendly.

'Any comment, Alex?'

'On what?'

'The meeting that's just been held.'

'I don't know anything about a meeting.'

'On your midnight escapade?'

'My *what*?'

'Gallivanting, so they say. There's talk of disciplinary action.'

I was speechless. Utterly. Then I heard myself say, cold and supercilious as a fish, 'I have no comment. I have a race in ten minutes and I'd be obliged if you'd leave me alone.'

'You mean to say you didn't know about the meeting?' I knew that look, amused, wicked, so full of malice. He knew I didn't. Coming from an evening paper, he wanted a quick quote, a good strong reaction from me to whip up a story before his mid-day deadline. I'd learnt a few things at last. As I turned away, staring at the race that was in progress, he went on, 'I gather there was some doubt as to whether you'd be allowed to swim this morning.'

'Go away.' I could have been a lot ruder. When he didn't, I got up and moved, catching Maggie's eye—

such a strange expression, half pleading, half pity, trying to tell me something but this was neither the time nor the place.

Maggie's heat was called. She did a great sixty-five point six seconds, a national record. In the sunshine, surging through the still water, it looked so easy, effortless, beautiful. She was roundly applauded. By this time I was as angry as I'd ever been in my life. Allowed or not, I'm here, I'm swimming and nothing and nobody will stop me! I stood on the block with my head lowered, feeling like a clap of thunder. I swam the race in a fury, oblivious of the other girls, finishing about three seconds clear. When I looked up my timekeepers were grinning and nodding at me like a pack of demented monkeys—sixty-five point two. I'd gone one better, and broken her record.

No, please, no. I don't want it, not now. It will hang around me like a dead weight in the final to-night. I'd never yet done a good final after a fast heat. Heats didn't matter a damn, it was only the final that counted, in the end. And now I'll be in the wrong lane, the blind lane.

I climbed from the pool, feeling sick. People said great swim, and clapped me on the back, but I could only think of getting to the sheds. I gathered up my towel and track suit and ran. A photographer tried to take a picture, but I ignored him.

In the toilet, I was violently ill. I stayed there, until the shaking had at last started to subside. Outside, I heard the usual chatter of competitors coming and going. Mrs Hooper's voice called 'Alex? Alex, are you all right?' 'Yes,' was enough to send her away. I was so cold.

'Alex?' I recognized Carol's voice. 'Alex, you in there?'

'Yes.'

'Message from your Dad. Great swim. Please join him as soon as possible.'

Too right I'll join him, and Mr Jack, and find out what's going on. I caught a glimpse of myself in the mirror as I came out, and wished I hadn't. Then I saw Maggie, clearly waiting for me. She beckoned me into a narrow passageway between two sets of lockers.

'Alex, that was a great time.'

'Thanks.' What was all the secrecy?

'I won't get another chance.'

'To do what?'

She looked very uncomfortable. 'Well, before to-night . . . if I'd known what it'd lead to, I'd have stopped her, somehow.'

'I don't understand.'

'Reporting you to the manager for being out with Mr Phillips.'

'Mr who?'

'Mr Phillips, the pool manager.'

'Is that his name?'

'You don't know his name?'

'Of course I don't. I never even spoke to him until last night. Well, hardly. Just hello, goodbye, that sort of thing.'

'Then what . . . ? Mother was awake standing at the window having a cigarette. She gets nervous for me, you know. (Really?) She saw the car, you waved goodbye, he drove off tooting. That's what she felt she had to tell Mr Upjohn. Upholding team reputation, all that stuff. I did try to tell her it was none of our business. After all, if you wanted to spoil your chances by . . .'

'Listen, Maggie. I was having nightmares, real shockers, you know? Perhaps you don't. I was desperate enough to go for a walk, desperate for a swim to try to calm down before someone took me away in a straitjacket. You know that feeling, you need water, it's like you're addicted to it?'

She nodded.

'I saw a light on in the pool. Mr Phillips was there, checking something in the office, the till or something. He takes his job seriously, you've seen that. He'd just come from the officials' party and didn't need much persuading. It's his pool, he's the manager. I had a short swim, in the moonlight. It was great. I had togs on, it was all very proper. He offered to run me back to the motel, but I walked. He was just checking that I got home safely. I did, and I got about two hours' sleep last night. That's all.'

She didn't say anything. Then Maggie did something that gave me hope, whatever happened in the final, even if her mother succeeded in having me 'disciplined' and my name smeared, and my hopes for Rome dashed. She stepped forward and we embraced for a long understanding moment. A couple of juniors happened to pass the end of the passageway and stood there with their mouths open at what must have been the touching sight of two great rivals hugging like sisters. I couldn't give a damn who saw us, or what they thought of the fact that both of us were crying.

'Good luck, Alex,' she whispered. I knew she didn't mean for the race itself, but for that other battle, against people, hypocrisy, jealousy, pomposity and gossip. She wanted a fair fight tonight, and so did I. I heard Mrs Hooper's voice again, calling me, and the moment was over.

It was no doubt already all over the pool, this lie about my gallivanting. Feeling like death, I walked boldly out along the concourse, to where Dad, Gran and Mr Jack were sitting. 'Congratulations,' followed me all the way, and a few whispers too.

They looked very serious.

'Great swim, Alex,' Mr Jack said finally. 'Just great.'

'Then why aren't you celebrating,' I said bitterly. 'Do you believe what they've told you?'

'No.'

'Good. Because if they've told you I was out having some sort of date with Mr Phillips they've got it all wrong.'

'Keep your voice down, Alex,' said Dad.

'I'll tell you what happened.' I did, just as I had told Maggie. They looked relieved, amused, despairing all at once. I think Mrs Benton had overplayed her hand, because it seemed I'd actually been seen getting out of the car, and the toots (plural) had been loud enough to wake Maggie, which was, according to Mrs Benton, an unacceptable form of gamesmanship. From her, that was rich!

But I had to eat some humble pie. Even if I wasn't actually out painting the town red, I'd still been out doing something I ought not to. Little girl swimmers of fifteen shouldn't be out of their safe little beds at midnight.

'Well, where do we go from here?' said Mr Jack, sounding rather weary. 'I had hell's own job persuading them that you had to be allowed to swim in the heats. There would have been a full-blown scandal otherwise, which would obviously have rebounded on them when they heard the true facts. One or two were all for suspending you then and there.'

'Without hearing my side of the story?'

'Yes.'

'But that's a kangaroo court.'

'Alex, sit down,' said Dad.

Mr Jack actually laughed. 'True, Alex, Cecil Upjohn as judge, jury and executioner. But don't underestimate his power. I've got a lot of talking to do. I've got to get alongside Ron Phillips quick. I want you to get out of the way, and say nothing to nobody.'

'But . . .'

'Better still, Jim, Mrs Young. Take her away in the car. Out to Cape Kidnappers, anywhere. No, that's too far, but you know what I mean. Go to the Saturday afternoon flicks if it's the only way you can relax, take your mind off things. Anything!'

I sat silently. I wasn't to be allowed to speak for myself.

'Don't you trust me, Alex?'

'It's not that.'

'What is it then?'

'Just, well, I got myself into this mess . . . Surely all I have to do is explain . . .'

'And this time you've got to trust me to get you out of it. Explaining is not enough. You need Ron Phillips to back up your story. You'll need to eat a bit of humble pie about going for walks in the middle of the night. You're not the first young swimmer to fall foul of officials, you know. They know all about it in Aussie, and I wasn't born yesterday. I know what drove you to the pool last night. I wish to God you hadn't. But you did, and now I'm going to find Ron, so get lost, both of you, pronto. Excuse me, Mrs Young,' he said, with a momentary twinkle at Gran.

'T.T.F.N.,' I said, rather naughtily under the circumstances.

'Get out of here. By the way, I reckon you'll both break the record again tonight. But you'll crack it the most. Now get.'

I love you, Mr Jack. Gold in record time. You still have faith I can do it, despite everything.

It was a long long day. We went back to the motel. I changed from track suit into the jeans I wore most of the time now. We went for a little walk into town because I had to find a dairy that sold what I needed for a period coming a week earlier than expected.

The ache in my tum had gone, but it had been nothing compared to the sick feeling I now had to live with. I had two battles on my hands: one only I could win, one I must trust someone else to win for me.

Lunch in a hotel was subdued and I had to force myself to eat the steak and mashed potato I knew I had to eat. Tonight I'd be down to glucose tablets. Gran and Dad talked about the old days, the people she'd been visiting during the week; it was like a conversation overheard in a bus, not quite understood.

We bought some orchard fruit, peaches and watermelon, and ate them on the return journey, finishing up on Bluff Hill, the headland overlooking the port and beach front. Dad got Gran talking, this time about the great earthquake of 1931 when large bits of land rose from the sea and others fell into it, and the whole central city area was wrecked. Gran's story was gloomy, because Albert's shop had been completely destroyed and their house damaged. Lots of people, about two hundred and fifty, had died the day it happened, buried, burned, trapped, many known to Gran, or children or parents of her friends. Today, in the sunshine, it looked like a sleepy seaside town with a small port and a nice waterfront.

Time dragged. I rejected the idea of a Saturday matinee, the aquarium, going back to the hotel for a rest. I wanted a quiet beach, shaded, cool, away from people, which we found to the north of Bluff Hill. Dad miraculously produced a lilo out of the car and blew it up, and Gran threatened me with a smacked bottom if I did not rest on it. Sounds of seagulls, children and the sea lulled me into a deep dreamless sleep for nearly two hours. I woke feeling woozy, but I was over the worst of the waiting period, and after that things began to improve.

Around five thirty we went back to the hotel, to find a note left at the desk by Mr Jack.

'All's well. Complaint dropped. For Pete's sake Alex, *don't* talk to any reporters. See you for tea, 6 pm.'

I looked at Dad. If I looked half as relieved as he did . . . I could only grin feebly. He just shook his head, despairingly. 'I don't know, Alex. Always skating on thin ice.'

I would meet Maggie tonight, in a fair fight. A reporter, my malicious friend from the morning session, turned up and was firmly told by Dad I had nothing to say.

When Mr Jack joined us in the dining-room he was grinning from ear to ear. Over a large mixed grill, while I toyed with an omelette, he explained that my friend Mr Phillips had been as outraged as me, when he heard what was being hinted at behind the closed doors of the committee room. He had his own reputation as pool manager at stake. It was his first such job and he didn't intend to let some gossiping woman and a self-righteous official ruin him. So, of course, his story tallied exactly with mine, and I knew I had been wrong to suspect his motives for offering me a lift home.

'They accepted his explanation. I think they even learnt something about the pressures swimmers can get under. He told them, when you appeared in the office, you looked like a ghost. He seriously thought you were on the verge of a breakdown. A quick dip, if that was all you wanted, seemed a simple enough way of getting you back on the rails. He'd intended to have a word with me in the morning. When you powered off to a new national record there didn't seem to be much point.'

Curtain down on another saga. I seem to attract attention, trouble, gossip, talk. Was it always going to be like this?

'The dreams. Were they that bad, Alex?' Dad said gently.

'Yeah.'

'Do you want to tell us?'

'No.' The images had already faded, and I had no intention of trying to pull them back into focus. What I needed now was some time to myself. 'Excuse me, I'll be back, half an hour.'

They did not follow me. Our room was empty. Carol had finished her events and was away having fun. On the dressing-table was a huge pile of telegrams: from Mum and the kids, from Miss Gillies, staff and pupils; from Miss Macrae (Go, and catch a falling star [John Donne] Marcia Macrae); from Julia, and other classmates; from Auntie Pat and Uncle Ernie; from Miss de Latour who had never forgiven me for growing so tall; from my piano teacher; and incredibly even one from Keith! There were telegrams from relatives I barely knew and the neighbours on both sides and several up and down the street as well, and some of Gran's friends who we visit each Christmas. So many people taking the trouble!

One of the last I opened read, 'To a true champion, our thoughts and love, from Tom and Elizabeth Richmond.' I lay on the bed, looking at it with wet eyes, for quite a time.

It is time to go. I get up, and under the shower wash my hair. It will be wet again soon, but I must be shining clean for the moment when I strip my track suit off, stand on the block, face my audience and my opponent and my task.

This is opening night, this my dressing-room. Instead of the costume of another identity, the make-up that hides, and changes, I am paring myself down to essentials. Slowly, with care, I shave armpits and legs, even thighs and arms below my elbows, which is something I've not done before. I must be sleek as a dolphin. Before the mirror I stand for just a moment: I see a lean female body, with small firm breasts, a flat stomach, wide shouders, eyes a bit wild, cheeks a bit gaunt. I look fit, battle-scarred, prepared.

Around my neck is Andy's single pearl, a tear-drop.

My costume is a pair of practice togs for warm-up, track suit, although the night is warm. Carefully packed along with towels, caps, glucose and tampons are my precious togs saved for tonight, for luck. I also pack a dress, petticoat and shoes, because there is usually a party on the last night.

I wonder how Maggie is feeling. Then I think of her mother and one or two others who've directly tried to cut me down to size, to be the also-ran, the normal teenage feminine girl, and a few more who've tried indirectly, and I allow myself a big broad smile.

My stomach is churning, my hands are even trembling a little as I comb my hair, but above all that, I feel tall, strong, invincible. I stand for a last moment, savouring the peace of being with myself. Once I close the door of Room Seven behind me, I become public property. There will be the quiet anxious faces of Dad and Gran and Mr Jack, reporters, photographers, all those people, a glimpse of Mrs Benton, the awareness of Maggie. I fold up the Richmond telegram and put it in my track suit pocket, next to my heart.

Lead on, Andy. I'm ready.

Epilogue

I'm nine years old and it's my first race again and I'm swimming so fast that I try to swim right through the end of the pool.

Two strokes, one. I'm swimming up a waterfall. I'm at the bottom of the sea. I've drowned.

I've touched, with an arm I swear grew five inches. Later I'll find all my fingers are bruised.

All movement stops. It has stopped in the next lane too, where Maggie lies on her back gasping like a fish in extremis. I can hear nothing, see nothing. I hang over the lane ropes. I will never swim another race as long as I live. I don't think I'll survive to tell the tale.

Gradually, I'm aware of a crowd on its feet, applause, cheering; thankfully, because my body is making most peculiar noises as I draw in great lungfuls of air. I am strangely uninterested in the result.

Liar, he says. Anyway, you know, don't you?

Do I? Dare I?

Yes, you'll dare anything now.

It was supposed to be my gift to you.

It was. You gave me yourself, the greatest gift of all. Now stand up. You're the champ. Enjoy the rituals. Maggie wants to congratulate you. You can

*enjoy being friends now. You're both going to Rome,
you know, but don't tell her just yet.*

You knew? All the time?

Of course.

Through all that? Killing myself . . . You knew?

*My gift was hope. Arrivederci. I loved you, sweet
maid . . .*

Andy?

Arrivederci . . .

Before you leave me, I love you too . . .

ABOUT THE AUTHOR

Tessa Duder, once a New Zealand representative swimmer, was record holder for butterfly and medley, and won a silver medal at the 1958 British Empire Games. *In Lane Three, Alex Archer* was named the New Zealand Children's Book of the Year in 1988, a 1989 ALA Best Book for Young Adults, and was awarded the Esther Glen Medal by the New Zealand Library Association. Her second novel, *Jellybean,* was an American Library Association Notable Book for 1986. Tessa Duder lives in Auckland, New Zealand, where she writes full-time.

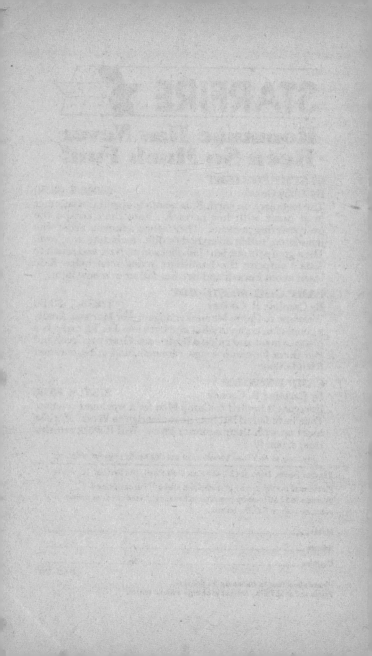